Death of the Mystery Novel

Also by Robert Underhill

Strawberry Moon
Cathead Bay

Death of the Mystery Novel

Robert Underhill

delicti press

Northport, Michigan

Death of the Mystery Novel

ISBN 10: 9798526-1-7
ISBN 13: 978-0-9798526-1-9
PCN 2008930885

Delicti Press
Northport, Michigan
editor@delictipress.com

This is a work of fiction. Names, character, places and incidents are either products of the author's imagination or are used fictitiously.

Publisher's Cataloging-in-Publication
      Underhill, Robert
      p.cm.
      ISBN: 13 978-0-9798526-1-9
      ISBN: 10 0-9798526-1-7

      1. Ann Arbor--University of Michigan—Fiction
      2. Detective and mystery stories I.Title

For Jim and Sue of Thayer Street

Acknowledgements

I got more than a little help from my friends: Trudy Carpenter, Kathleen Snedeker, Nancy Terfertiller, and John and Michelle Underhill. Thanks for the time and serious thought you gave to this project.

1

Byron Page looked out on a magical scene. Eight inches of the lightest, most crystalline snow had fallen so gently during the night that the flakes remained perfect. They flashed in the morning sun as countless prisms. Standing at the open doorway after picking up his *Times*, he watched three students walk by kicking up puffs of powder while calling across the street to friends, spontaneous delight in their voices. A rare moment. Soon the wind and spray from cars would round the perfection down to an ordinary, snowy scene—still beautiful, but not magical. How many more perfect moments in a lifetime? Few, Byron thought, few and evanescent. The mind is thrilled, the moment passes, and afterward memory can't recreate it. He thought now of Cara, wishing she were here with him to share this moment. Her damned pager had gone off last night as they were about to go to bed and she'd gone off to Police Headquarters and hadn't returned.

This was Ann Arbor and what he could see, standing at his home on Thayer Street, was the northwest corner of the University of Michigan's main campus. Byron had been living in his renovated house for only six months. The bronze centennial plaque next to the entrance said it was the "Hutchinson House—1896." A residence when built, it had then served many commercial needs until Byron bought it.

He'd gotten it for a decent price in this insanely overpriced city, because a group of psychologists, who had divided the interior into small individual offices, decided to split. The group's dissolution presented Byron with the opportunity. Money inherited from his maiden aunt, Mildred, provided the means . . . well, most of it. There was the usual overrun on the renovation.

A more perfectly located abode was hard to imagine. His office and the classrooms were an easy walk. Two coffee shops and a bar a mere block away. Bookstores were a block and a half and the gym and pool used by the faculty twice that distance. Cara's office at Police Headquarters was exactly eight minutes on foot if you didn't stop to talk to a colleague or to look at the tweed sport coats in Van Boven's window, which meant he and Cara lunched together most days. The convenient location also meant she could easily be talked into staying the night rather than driving the twenty minutes to her place in Dexter, a house she shared with Jocelyn Jackson, the women's gymnastic coach. Normally a woman might worry these violent days if her housemate didn't come home at night, but Jocie was used to it and knew that Cara, being a cop, never went anywhere without her gun—make that weapon.

Byron walked back along the bare maple floor of the hallway to the kitchen and put the kettle on the enormous Viking gas range he'd had installed. The commercial grade stove had cost a small fortune. Proof of Cara's empathic nature was the fact that she hadn't laughed out loud when she'd first seen it. Considering that Byron only had four dishes in his repertoire and that he never cooked for more than three couples at a time, the extravagant purchase warranted the question put to him by the deliveryman, "Opening a restaurant?"

He was sensitive about the stove and after a jibe about it by his best friend, Andy Backus, he'd snapped back sharply, "Shouldn't one at least be able to break a hundred before dropping two grand for a set of Calloway clubs?" Hearing of this exchange, and being afraid their own foibles would also be cataloged, other friends had quickly shut up about the stove.

He put an English muffin in his new industrial strength British toaster that scorned the modernity of popping up, and got a jar of Pam Backus's homemade currant jam out of the refrigerator. He was thinking of Cara and wondering what had kept her away all night. She'd said the page had been for a routine matter, but since she was on first call, she had to go in. She'd left saying she'd be back in half an hour. Well, he thought, nothing takes only half an hour even if it should. Whatever the problem, it probably had dragged on until the wee hours and not wanting to disturb him, she had gone on home. Or maybe she had gone home because she was dead tired and didn't want *him* to disturb *her*. She would have been right about that.

In the midst of his musing the phone rang and he picked up the receiver thinking he was about to find out the answer. "What happened?" he said.

After a short pause, Andy Backus's amused voice asked, "You're not dying are you?"

"Dying?"

"Well, you know Gertrude Stein's final words were, 'What was the question?' I know you'd try to be original."

Today was Friday and on Fridays Andy usually came by for a cup of coffee before his nine o'clock class. Byron's Friday was free until he met with a graduate student at ten.

Andy went on, "Now you'd only answer the phone as you just did if you were expecting the call to be from a certain police sergeant, which means she's not there with you and the coast is clear for me to get my coffee."

"The kettle's almost boiling," Byron answered and hung up. He was pretty sure the call had been made on Andy's cell phone and probably from less than a block away.

Byron knew what would be on Andy's mind this morning—Dennis Duke. Although Andy was one of the most neutral members of the English Department on the subject of the sellingest writer in America, he would be fully wound-up and eager to talk about the guy.

Four months ago, faced with the need to find a new chairman, two opposing factions in the English Department, each unable to force its own candidate on the other, had settled on a safe compromise, Henry Beasley. Henry, who had two years remaining before the age of forced retirement, was selected and the university administration acquiesced. Henry's two years at the helm were calculated to give the warring factions time to regroup and maneuver for eventual victory. Henry could be relied upon to be a benign caretaker. He had quietly and uncomplainingly taught freshman composition and introduction to the novel for so many years that he had become as tolerantly accepted—and overlooked— as the monthly faculty tea, a gathering, incidentally, that Henry never missed.

What no one expected was that Henry had some ideas

of his own. He had attended the University of Georgia as an undergraduate and had been strongly impressed (as only the young can be) with their library's boast of having the world's most complete collection of mystery novels. Now looking back over the years, there had been a sure sign, had anyone paid attention, of what was to occur once Henry was in charge. The warning was there for anyone who recognized that Henry's regular inclusion of a mystery novel in his novels course wasn't a joke.

On the occasion of the very first departmental meeting which Henry chaired, he made the astonishing announcement that the current, popular bestseller was, *ipso facto,* the standard of literature of its age. He quickly cited Shakespeare and Dickens before hurrying on to let all those present know that he was inviting half a dozen or more mystery and thriller authors whose books dominated bookstore and drug store shelves to lecture at the university. All of the English faculty would be required to be present and to also attend the dinner to be given in honor of each guest. He then revealed the names of those to whom he had already sent invitations. If one had to find one word to describe the general reaction of the faculty it was "disbelief". For many it was "nausea". There was no protest—they all realized they had brought it on themselves.

Dennis Duke was the first invitee. Yesterday, he had given his lecture and last night the whole English faculty obligingly—or guiltily—sat down to sup with the reigning king of the horror novel.

The doorbell rang and Byron let Andy in.

"I've wondered how it would have felt to be a German museum curator when the Nazis redefined art and told you what was now acceptable to display and what had to come off the walls," Andy said before he even shed his coat.

"It probably opened up a lot of wall space," Byron observed.

"Exactly. No matter that you hated to comply, it was damn certain you would."

"Probably. Your point?"

Andy gestured for patience. "Now, this guy Duke is obviously suffering from a bad case of childhood fear of what was under his childhood bed and we sat there last night and let him pass his inspiration off as . . . what was it? Oh yeah, 'a reflection of man's own fear of his sins against God and nature.' If that isn't a load of horse manure, and yet we all sat quietly and acted like we bought it!"

Byron led Andy back to the kitchen where he pushed the plunger down on the coffee maker and put another muffin in the toaster. "Do you deny that he builds incredible tension in his writing?"

"No," snapped Andy, "And watching a guy about to jump off a building also builds tension, but it's not literature."

Byron, playing the gadfly replied, "Our Lord and master, Henry Beasley, would say you are defining literature by antiquated standards. Dennis Duke sells *muchos libros.*"

"You're just trying to goad me. I know for a fact you don't believe that's an indication of a book's worth. But as you know I could give a shit about how many books Duke sells. Having no ambition to write anything except—following the example of your success with your aunt—my monthly bonding letter to my rich uncle, I'm free from the natural envy that the would-be novelists in our department all have. You, of course, are also beyond envy having had all the publishers on earth beg to be chosen to bring out your new book." Andy accompanied this compliment with a bow. "No, what bothers me is this 'sins against God and nature' crap, that's all."

"You'll have to fill me in on departmental envy. I've been . . ."

"I know, covering the police beat," Andy interjected. He was smiling broadly, blue eyes bright behind steel rimmed glasses, full cheeks flushed by the kitchen's warmth.

"Yours," he continued, "is a much better assignment, believe me, but let's see, what can I tell you about the department? Jack Sumner's publisher rejected his latest effort. The book is, according to Ruth Hackett, who did some editing for him, a highly convoluted search for sexual identity. Although they had published his two previous books, Thornberry Press sent him a rather impersonal letter of rejection—the 'Not suited for our list' type of thing. He called and found out that his former editor now owns an oxygen bar at Kennedy Airport and the guy he talked to allowed that searches for sexual identity are a thing of the past. These days it's well known that it's all genetically determined and your nearest geneticist is better qualified than a novelist to help with a search, should you need it, which you shouldn't, because nobody gives a damn anymore. Jack is furious. He hates Dennis Duke because, and I quote, 'The tripe he writes shrinks reader's minds to walnut size!'

"More envy . . . let's see . . . " Andy tapped his forehead as if to jog loose a thought. "The Three Musketeers Schlink, Sheets and Sleeves, are our local members of the 'composite

7

novel' school. They write a novel together, only they don't communicate with each other during the process. The reader has to buy all three books and read them simultaneously and construct 'the novel' in his or her own mind. I hear they owe the publisher money on their last effort.

"Anyway, it is rumored that the Musketeers have formed a pact—mingling of blood and that sort of thing—to kill Duke and all the other mega-sales novelists who are slated to come here. They look upon Beasley's chairmanship as a heaven sent sign that these philistines are being delivered into their hands for the purpose of execution."

Byron considered this with a worried look.

"Don't worry," Andy said in a reassuring tone, "They talk, but they would be the last to take any kind of action—I think."

"It's not that," Byron said. "It just occurred to me that it would be dangerous to mingle blood with Sleeves. And by the way, I don't want to hear that you've been spreading rumors that I worked at getting my aunt to leave me her estate. That's not the way it was at all. Aunt Mildred and I were bonded when I was but a mewling babe."

Andy shot back, "So you started early. It's a little late for me to mewl, so I have to write endearing letters to my uncle." Then fixing Byron with a quizzical look, he added, "A bit touchy this morning, aren't we? What happened last night, did she get mad and go home?"

Byron smiled, "You got it half right. She was called to perform her duty for us citizens."

"I see." Andy was silent for a few moments before continuing. "OK, I've reported on the flow of the faculty undercurrent. What was *your* impression of Dennis the Duke?"

Byron shrugged. "He scares the bejesus out of people as much as any rollercoaster. People are eager to pay for either of those rides."

"What about the 'sins against God and Nature' malarkey?"

"OK. But, don't quote me. He's not a bad writer. However, he creates tension by one method alone: he dreams up something weird and dreadful with which to scare the reader, caring little if it makes sense, or has a reasonable explanation in the end. As you said, he recreates the kind of experience a child may have. The kid is scared to death of what might be under the bed and runs to the parents. Only he finds the parents aren't in their room where they should be and so the fear increases and he runs downstairs. My God, they're not there either and isn't the living room couch moving strangely and menacingly toward the kid? Now terrified out of his or her mind the kid runs out of the house into the night, only to discover mom and dad right there in the family car looking for mom's earrings. Relief follows, however it's not the relief that comes with problem-solving following a development of character, but only an immature feeling of safety in the parents' presence. I think you're right, that's what Duke is doing, finding that immature safety for himself over and over again . . . plus the security of building up an enviable bank balance."

Andy was happy with Byron's agreement. "Well put, but I didn't hear you saying any of this in the discussion period last night."

"And I didn't hear you."

Andy smiled slyly. "But, I'm only a grubbing researcher cataloging obscure examples of narrative style in the eighteenth century novel. You, as the Humphrey Professor of Shakespeare, should be the vigilant defender of the art of literature against its eroding debasement by the likes of Dennis Duke."

"You really think so? Well, as a matter of fact, I stole out last night and murdered him in his sleep before the Three Musketeers could get a chance. I put the poor devil out of his misery."

"Way to go! Why didn't you say so in the first place?" Andy drummed his fingers and looked wistful. "I wish I'd thought of doing that, instead I went home from that dinner with indigestion."

"I also felt peckish when I left the dinner, but then I came across all those students building that gigantic snowman on the Diag. Did you see it?"

Andy shook his head.

"The biggest one I've ever seen. It must be thirty feet high. There were at least fifty of them working on it and having a grand old time. I stood and watched and as I did my discomfort went away. They had built a ramp just like the Egyptian pyramid builders in order to roll the upper torso and the head into place. A black plastic garbage can with an added cardboard brim became the hat. This was hoisted up using a vaulting pole that they, then, gave him to hold. Take a detour on your way to your class and have a look."

"Maybe I'll stop and add some finishing touches instead of going to the class."

The phone rang.

"Could this be our protector of the public's safety?" quipped Andy.

"Could be. Hello . . . Oh yeah? I want to see the log sheet that backs you up . . . You're kidding . . . The gas station right there on Main and Huron? . . . At his brother-in-law's? Talk about stupid! What a waste of a smart detective. So, why didn't you come on back here? . . . What?" Byron's expression became one of shocked disbelief. "And, you've no idea? And, still no sign . . . " Byron listened without interrupting. "OK, I'll see you later. Sweet dreams."

Byron put down the phone and looked at his friend. "Dennis Duke is missing."

2

The houses along Evans Street were single story, wood-framed and old. They stood on lots too narrow to allow a driveway to squeeze between them. Although it was the end of January, here and there Christmas lights still adorned a tree or outlined a window. The snowplow had just made a run down the street piling the new snow so high on top of the existing bank that Hank Kelly was forced up out of his slouch in the squad car's passenger seat to see the house numbers. He shoved a potato chip in his mouth and through the crunch announced, "Three forty, it's in the next block."

Cara Bartoli was at the wheel. Sandy Dorsey, the other woman detective in the department, had to fight with her partner for equal driving time. Equal time was something a woman had to insist on or she'd quickly be classified as gofer material. Cara didn't have that problem with Hank; he preferred to have both hands free for eating.

Actually Cara outranked him—for the past two months. She was now a sergeant. She'd wondered how her promotion might affect their relationship and so far she could detect none. He'd said, "Way to go kid," when he'd first heard and he'd bought her a Dove bar to celebrate.

Cara was in no mood to be pursuing the stupid jerk who'd robbed the downtown Shell station. When she'd left Byron and trudged through the snow to headquarters she expected to sign a prisoner's transfer form (one which should have been signed on the earlier shift) and be back beside him in bed in under thirty minutes. That timing turned out to be about right, but as she turned to head back to the pleasures of Thayer Street, the call came in that the gas station had just been held up. Based on the information taken by the desk sergeant, an APB was immediately put out on a red Ford pickup. Cara, disappointed but resigned, rousted Hank and they began their investigation.

It turned out to be a laugher. The unmasked robber had shown the young female clerk that he had a gun in his pocket and demanded all the cash—$112. He then picked up two cans of brake fluid and left, leaving his prints on everything. The clerk remembered seeing WGH on the license plate, but didn't remember the numbers. That meant it took an extra four seconds for the state computer to tell them there was only one Ford pickup truck in Washtenaw County with a plate number beginning WGH, a 1988 F-100 registered to Willard Hissup on Pontiac Trail.

"We don't even need the address," Hank said when they left the gas station. "We can drive around and look for a red pick-up parked over a puddle of brake fluid. "

When the name and address had come through from the state computer, Cara opened the phone book, ran her finger down the page and read out the name, Frank Hissup. "Must be his parent's house." She thought a moment then added, "It's like this, his father's dead, but the mother keeps the old man's name in the book. Willard lives . . . No, Willard and his wife live with her. But, he won't be there. He's too smart for that, right? He'll be at his wife's sister's house."

Cara's eyes always communicated a deep and dedicated friendliness—even when dealing with the likes of a Willard Hissup. But as she looked over at her partner after making her prediction there was also challenge in the look. Hank noted it.

"OK," he said, "You're on for five bucks."

"Like candy from a baby."

"How you gonna locate this sister-in-law?"

Cara began dialing. "I'll just call Ma Hissup and ask her."

The arrest was almost embarrassing. Willard's brother-in-law answered the door. Willard, his wife Debbie and her sister Darla were sitting in the tiny living room drinking beer and watching an old movie. Cara's announcement that she and Hank were Ann Arbor police, brought forth a spontaneous, "Oh, shit," of disgust from the two women. Willard had screwed up again.

Hank put the docile Willard in the back seat and handed Cara five dollars when he got in beside her. In order to soften his loss, he threw in a jibe, "That was quick, the night's young and you still have time to bed the bard."

Hank was a good guy and she was sure, after working with him for more than a year, that he really respected her, but there were times when he went too far. Her sex life was on the other side of the line.

She pretended to applaud and said, "Bard? That's very good . . . for you. You must have sneaked off again to read *Classic Comics*."

Hank knew he'd gone too far. Cara could turn on you like a damn cobra and he also knew he wasn't her equal in mental fencing. He threw up his hands. "I'm sorry. You win."

Hank, however, had put into words exactly what she'd been thinking; she couldn't wait to slide between the sheets and into Byron's arms. She handed Hank the mandatory paperwork on Hissup. He took it without complaint, knowing his acknowledged transgression now included obligatory grunt work. Cara was again about to leave the building when the desk sergeant asked her to pick up line three.

"Detective Sergeant Bartoli speaking," she said.

"Detective Bartoli, this is Harrison Finch. I'm the business manager for Dennis Duke." He announced this as if there could be no living human who was unfamiliar with the name and importance of Dennis Duke. "Mr. Duke is missing. He was supposed to meet with me at eleven-thirty in his hotel lobby after the dinner the English Department held in his honor. He never came. I called his room several times and finally persuaded the hotel manager to go up there and check. Mr. Duke wasn't there and his bed had not been used. It is now one o'clock and I'm very concerned."

Cara thought for a moment. "Have you known Mr. Duke long, Mr. Finch?"

"I'd say so. I began working for him after *Screaming*. That was fourteen books ago, you know."

"Then, I take it, this is unusual behavior for Mr. Duke?"

"Very."

"It's rather a beautiful snowfall tonight, might he be out for a walk?"

"Possibly—if someone were with him whom he knew well. Mr. Duke never goes out after dark by himself."

"I see. And, there's no one beside yourself whom he

knows well here in Ann Arbor?"

"No one." Thinking that the woman detective was not taking his concern seriously enough, he added, "I needn't remind you that Mr. Duke is a very important person."

He'd said she needn't be reminded, but then he'd reminded her. Cara heard the threat. She was very sure that Dennis Duke was a very important person—to Harrison Finch's personal finances at least.

"You're at his hotel now?"

"Yes."

"The Bell Tower Hotel?"

It was a favorite place to lodge visiting dignitaries and located only half a block from Byron's house on Thayer Street.

"Yes."

"I'll be there in ten minutes."

•　•　•

"What do you mean he's missing?" asked Andy, frozen in the act of sipping his coffee.

"Cara said his business manager reported that Duke wasn't in his room at 1 a.m. She went over to the Bell Tower Hotel and questioned the staff and found one person who'd seen him going out alone shortly before eleven. He hasn't been seen since."

"Huh. What do you suppose happened?"

"Dunno. Maybe a secret assignation. Any opinion about his sexual preference?"

"Werewolves."

Byron laughed. "There are certainly a lot of those around here—half a dozen in the Psychology Department alone."

"He doesn't strike me as the kind of guy who would have lustful urges—not a Mailer type, if you know what I mean. I think all of his sexual life is right there in those scary fantasies of his."

"OK, then, maybe he was kidnapped for ransom."

"That would be a damn risky thing to do. I mean his readers are so avid they would tear anyone apart who caused a moment's delay in the issue of his next book."

"No doubt," Byron said, "there will be a benign reason in the end." He thought for a moment. "I hope to God that's the case. It would not be good for the university to have visiting dignitaries disappear from campus."

"Right. And poor old Beasley, this program of his is awful but he means well. I'd hate to see him feel responsible for harm coming to one of his guests." Andy finished his coffee and stood. "Cara was dealing with this all night?"

"Yes. She just went home to get some sleep."

"Does this now become her case?"

"Yes, I believe that's the way it works. Her partner will be watching the store until she gets twenty winks."

Andy donned his overcoat and pulled a wool stocking cap down over his balding head. "I have to admit that something like this is stimulating. I find myself going to my day's rounds with an unusual measure of excitement. Makes one realize that the daily contemplation of Fielding's use of irony has its limits. Tell me Byron, why *do* those students continue coming to class?"

Leaning heavily on his sonorous, bass-baritone Byron replied, "They're very young, my friend."

Alone, Byron poured another cup of coffee and went upstairs. His eye fell left and right with satisfaction on the large pieces of antique furniture he'd acquired from his aunt's estate. In his former, small apartment they had been crowded together like actors waiting in the wings. Now they enjoyed the space leading players deserved. He showered, shaved and was choosing a tie when Andy called, again.

"I see what you mean. That *was* the mother of all snowmen."

"Was?"

"Afraid so. There was a group of grieving students viewing the remains as I passed. The top of the body and the head took a tumble."

Byron groaned, "Ah, that's too bad. Too bad that everyone didn't get a chance to see him in his prime."

"We all have to go sometime."

3

Before taking their lunch break, the four-man crew from Buildings and Grounds decided to use the front-loader to scoop up the two huge snowballs from the sidewalk of the Diag, the sidewalk that diagonally cleaves the main campus into two triangles. So it was at precisely 12:06 that the body of Dennis Duke was discovered beneath the fallen snowman. A look of abject, wide-eyed terror was frozen on the famous writer's face. That fear, in turn, was communicated to the workmen, who stood paralyzed.

"One of the men said it looked to him as if the snowman had deliberately pounced on top of Duke," Cara remarked.

She and Byron were having an early dinner at his house. She had only managed to get three hour's sleep at the time Hank had called with this news. Her smooth, olive-toned face didn't show it. Byron was impressed with her resilience. He was only three years older than she, but he knew what he'd look like if he'd been up all night.

"At what time do you think it happened?" he asked.

"The Medical Examiner says it's pretty hard to determine exactly, because Duke was frozen right through. It's pretty clear he wasn't alive long after the thing fell on him. It's unlikely that we'll find a witness to the actual event, because that person would have gone for help. The stage of digestion of the free meal to which you guys had treated him would put death between eleven and midnight. We know the snowman was standing at ten-thirty. The next witness we've been able to locate, a security man making his rounds at one-twenty, saw that it had fallen."

"And you say one of the hotel staff saw Duke leaving the hotel just before eleven?"

Cara nodded as she put some spaghetti marinara in her mouth and sucked up an errant noodle. She glanced up to see Byron staring at her. She thought he was focused on her pasta technique. He, however, was just fascinated watching her. He loved the way her short, dark hair hugged her face like a pair of adoring hands. Everything about her was a wonder to him. He didn't want to appear to be an enthralled adolescent, so he hurried on.

"Damn strange for it to fall. There was no wind to speak of last night."

"This may explain it. There is something we learned about the building of the snowman." She paused a moment to check a number on her pager, then continued, "When the students had rolled the big upper body ball up along the ramp they'd built, they found they couldn't get enough people on the ramp to push it off and on top of the lower body. At that point, someone thought of throwing a plastic sheet over the larger, lower snowball to make it easier to slide the upper part onto it. Afterward, they trimmed the plastic away so it wouldn't show. An engineer I talked to thinks that just the slight jarring of the earth from students passing along the sidewalk could have caused it to gradually slide slowly forward on the plastic until it finally fell."

"Really? I didn't know about the plastic sheet. When I

came along it must already have been trimmed." He wondered to himself if he should have been more alert to the hazard potential of a thirty-foot snowman.

"This sauce is sooo good. Did you make this?"

"Wish I had," Byron answered. "Pam Backus sent it over." He teased a bright orange speck out of the sauce with his fork. "Carrots and all sorts of wonderful secret ingredients. But don't bother asking her for the recipe. It's a family secret whispered on the deathbed to the oldest daughter."

"Heya, thatsa righta." exclaimed Cara with the appropriate gestures God gave Italians.

"Anyway," she continued, "we've checked with the cab companies and no one picked him up at the hotel and no one arrived by cab at the hotel around eleven. He received no calls on the hotel lines and he made no calls. He did have a cell phone and while there is no record of his having made a call, someone may have called him. If one puts aside his business manager's claim that Duke never went outside alone after dark, a likely scenario is something like this. Duke went for a walk, discovered Mr. Snowman and stood looking up until he realized in a moment of terror that it was falling on him."

"You're satisfied, then, that it happened that way?"

Cara shrugged. "These dumb things are always happening. A guy digs a trench and it caves in on him. Another cuts down a tree and it falls on him. Also, the autopsy revealed no other cause of death except asphyxiation."

"I keep thinking that it's too much like something out of one of his books to be real. You know, like the thing that's always been chasing him finally caught him."

Cara stared at the cup she was turning slowly back

and forth on the tabletop. "Yeah, unfortunately it's very real and this Finch has already been in touch with Dennis Duke's lawyer and he in turn has a top gun litigator flying out here. The case is a liability dream. The university will have no defense."

"Too bad it's not murder. That would get the university off the hook."

The question of responsibility brought Henry Beasley to Byron's mind. The poor old guy must feel horrible. Byron decided he would run by Beasley's office the next morning and lend his support.

"I haven't completely ruled out murder, you know," Cara added while glancing at her watch and starting to rise. "Remember, I did say that it looks like an accident only if one puts aside the business manager's assertion that Duke would never go out alone at night. Finch was very adamant on that point. If Duke was such a scaredy-cat, then we have to wonder whom he met as he left the hotel."

Cara put their empty cups and plates into the sink then paused. "There is this other thing. Nothing really, but it nags."

"What's that?"

"I'm told when the students finished their work the snowman was holding a vaulting pole upright through the crook in its arm."

"That's right, I saw it."

"Well, you'd expect it to just fall over when the upper part of the body fell. The bottom end of the pole should have been near the base of the snowman and the pole should be lying in the same direction that the snowball fell, right?"

"So?"

"Well, it wasn't and it didn't. The whole pole was about ten feet behind the snowman."

Byron thought about this and began nodding.

"Also . . ."

"There's more?"

"Also there are faint indications of footprints by the pole. It continued to snow lightly until about midnight. The footprints the students had made were completely covered and obliterated. This means that someone walked behind the snowman at a later time than the students—say eleven—eleven-thirty."

"You're thinking someone could have helped the snowman fall?"

"Maybe made an appointment with Duke to meet at the snowman. Maybe hid behind it until Duke arrived and stood there innocently admiring it."

"Whoosh—plop. Farewell Dennis Duke."

"Could be."

"But, the footprints might have been made by anyone who came upon the snowy giant and circled it in awe."

"True. But, like I said, it nags."

• • •

Byron had to pause in the open doorway and regroup. He was expecting to find Henry Beasley a beaten man, bowed and humbled. Instead, there sat an invigorated Henry at his desk in the Department Chairman's office.

Beasley looked up, saw Byron and exclaimed brightly, "Ah, Page, I'm glad you're here. Dreadful thing about Dennis

Duke, but it justifies my new program, don't you think?"

Byron, who had anticipated an announcement of the cancellation of the best-selling author program, was dumbfounded.

"Er . . . ah ."

"Exactly. We got Duke here and recognized the serious value of his work just in the nick of time. Otherwise he would have passed on *sans* the wreath of the *literati* upon his brow." Beasley's pale blue eyes grew misty at the very thought.

Byron was stunned. "You're continuing the series, then?"

"Certainly! I've been busy this morning trying to move the dates up, so that we can get all the authors here before something happens to any of the rest of them. It's a dangerous world, you know." He looked at Byron for agreement.

"There is that." Byron didn't trust himself to say much and was looking for some graceful exit line. "Who then is to be the next guest?"

"I.B. Sames." Beasley said this with the tired impatience of a teacher who has to repeat the obvious to a dull pupil.

I.B. Sames fit the profile Beasley had in mind all right. Her latest book had a place on a bedside table in maybe one out of ten American homes. Byron had never read any of her stuff, but he knew of her popularity.

"Well then you must be busy. I'll just toddle off."

"I'm sure Sames must be your favorite of the current authors, being, I mean, so much like Shakespeare."

Byron couldn't control a gasp. "How's that?"

"She develops such strong female characters. Cut from the same cloth as Beatrice and . . . say Portia."

Byron was speechless.

"Something wrong, Page? You seem peaked. Perhaps you need some blood studies. Couldn't hurt, you know."

Byron knew he had to leave quickly. He hadn't had such an Alice-in-Wonderland feeling since that single time he'd dropped acid as a freshman.

"I need some sleep. Working late. I'll be off now." Byron spun on his heel and left.

Safely inside his own office, he reviewed the conversation with Beasley. Like Shakespeare? What in the world was in Beasley's mind? Strong female characters? He'd been told by a colleague that a few of I.B Sames's early books were very good, but the later ones were a tangle of words and senseless detail that entrapped one's consciousness so effectively that the mind surrendered in the end to sleep. "Like reading a catalog for an estate sale," his friend had said. Still, it made one curious. He would have to get a copy of one of her novels and glance through it. But how would he do that? He certainly didn't want it on record at the university library that he had checked out one of her books. He wondered if the library even owned one. He couldn't buy it at a bookstore either. Suppose one of his friends met him as he was leaving and asked, "What's that you're reading, Page?" He had an inspiration; Joan Arnold, the secretary he shared with Andy Backus and Ruth Hackett. He got up and went to her office.

Joan was busily typing. Sensing Byron's presence she threw a look in his direction over her half glasses.

"Yes?" she asked as her fingers continued to fly over the computer's keyboard and in a tone that said she expected his being there meant more work for her.

"Have you gone to lunch yet, Joan?"

"Just about to switch on the voice mail, why?"

I have a favor to ask." This would be hard to say. "Would you buy me a copy of er . . . ah . . . I.B. Sames's latest . . . ah, novel at the drug store?"

Alarmed surprise fell upon Joan. It was as if Byron had just announced that he was taking up cockfighting. Gradually she began to understand the situation. She couldn't let this opportunity pass without milking it to the limit.

"An unabridged edition, of course."

Byron understood he was going to have to run the gauntlet. He nodded.

"This is for a class assignment?"

"Ah, so you think it's a good idea, too?" He wouldn't be toyed with. "Which book do you suggest?"

"Actually, I read her last one . . . I think."

"What was it like? Strong female characters, right?"

Joan struggled to remember. "I, uh . . . I must have fallen asleep."

A lapse of memory wasn't like Joan. Like all secretaries she remembered more about your courses, students and the details of your publications than you could ever hope to remember yourself.

"OK, then any of her books will do," Byron said.

"But just a minute, Doctor Page, you really can't expect me to go into a store and ask to buy this kind of book. It's asking too much. I have *my* reputation to protect too. After all, I *am* a secretary in the English Department. I'd be more comfortable asking the clerk for DayGlow SuperTicklers. But, since it's for one of your classes, I'll make the sacrifice."

Byron opened his office door to hear the phone ringing.

"I thought I'd call to tell you it looks like you got your wish," Cara announced.

"My wish?"

"That Dennis Duke was murdered. I feel sure now it wasn't an accident."

"Really? How so?"

"I just got the report on the vaulting pole. I sent it to the lab first thing to check for fingerprints. There were none at all on about four feet of one end of the pole, but plenty on the rest of it."

Byron was straining to get the point so he wouldn't appear stupid.

"You don't get it do you? You see there should have been prints all over the pole from all those students who handled it. Why was four feet of the pole clean? Because someone wiped it clean. Why did he or she wipe it clean? Becau . . . "

"OK, OK," Byron interjected hurriedly, "I think I get it. But wait, those students must have been wearing gloves."

"OK, most were, but there were enough who weren't. The point is . . . "

"OK, OK."

"I thought you'd be happy. Since it wasn't caused by an accident, Duke's lawyers can't claim the university is liable."

"Yes, of course. Yes, murder. And a very unusual murder wouldn't you say? In fact a 'foul and most unnatural murder.'"

4

"From WHYY in Philadelphia, I'm Terry Gross and this is FR-E-S-H AIR.

"Normally we interview authors of recently published books. Today, our guest has become widely known for a book that won't be published for another five months. I'm speaking of Doctor Byron Page, the Humphrey Professor of Shakespeare at the University of Michigan. He is the author of three previous, highly respected works on the Shakespeare plays. The reason his new book is so eagerly awaited is because he claims he will reveal in it the name of the true author of the plays.

"His appearance on the show today is a preview, as it were, and he promises to come back after his book is published in June.

"Doctor Page, it's a special privilege to have you on the program in a very literal sense, because I understand this is the only interview you intend give before the publication of your book. Why is that and what is the book's title to be?"

"Terry, I consider it a special privilege to be on your program whatever the reason. It's true that I don't intend to participate in any media discussion of my book, *Please Let Me Introduce Mr. William Shakespeare,* before it's published. Unfortunately, this has caused many to suggest that I'm just playing hard to get. I've accepted your kind invitation to be on your program today, to explain myself. Terry. I'm not playing hard to get. I'm just afraid to be interviewed because I may say too much.

"You see, I have an agreement with my publisher that the name of the author of the plays won't be made known until the book is actually in bookstores."

"Is that to build suspense . . . and sales?"

"Suspense, yes. Sales, no. It's not my thinking, and I don't believe that of Cloistered Press either, that the total sales will be enhanced. The simple fact is this: Howard Forsythe at Cloistered and I are both hams. I can't resist a dramatic moment, and in my world, there has never been a more dramatic moment."

"You mean, the revelation of the name."

"Exactly. For centuries, certainly from as early as the late sixteen hundreds, the authorship has been questioned. As you know, many names of persons both well known and obscure have been put forward. Proof has always been lacking for unquestioned verification."

"Until now." There is a smile in Terry's voice.

Byron laughs. "Yes, until now."

"And you have unquestioned proof of identity?"

"I do. The embarrassing thing is that achieving this was not the result of long and diligent scholarship, which is what my university might prefer. It was just dumb luck. Last year, I was traveling in England, meeting with colleagues, doing a little research, being a tourist and so on, when quite unexpectedly I was asked to look at a number of documents that had been in the possession of a certain person's family since the early seventeenth century. It turns out, they were given to this person's ancestor for safe keeping by the author of the plays."

"There are so many questions that are flooding my mind right now."

"I'm sure there are, Terry. Who, what, when, why? And," Byron laughs, "I can't tell you."

"C'mon now."

"OK, I didn't come here entirely empty handed. I want to be invited back, after all.

"First, let me say that all the material has been exhaustively authenticated. Experts in dating archival material have examined it. Handwriting has been authenticated. The references to persons and events mentioned in the documents have been verified. There was even a play—previously unknown—among the papers. It was written before *The Tempest*.

"In short, this is not another theory of authorship. The mystery is over. I'm somewhat sad about that. It was a wonderful mystery, and now, alas, it *is* solved. I talked this over with Howard Forsythe at Cloistered Press and we've decided to say one thing—and it's partly to prepare some people who, I'm sorry to say, will no doubt suffer some injury from the revelation; I'm speaking of the people of Stratford-upon-Avon. I'm afraid they'll have to find a way to replace their former tourist income."

"Then, it's not the man from Stratford?"

"He's not the man.

"Terry, I said at the outset that I'm a pushover and not the equal of an interviewer like you, so before I say too much—and I'm afraid I went further than I intended with the mention of the new play—I'll be going. Thanks for having me on the show. I'll be back if you still want me after the release date in June."

"Come back coward! Well, I guess we'll have to wait like everyone else for the big day. Joseph Alton of the *New York Times* wrote recently, 'The greatest event in the history of publication in the English language occurred in 1623 with the publication of Shakespeare's First Folio of sixteen plays. The second greatest event will be the publication of *Please Let Me Introduce Mr. William Shakespeare.*'"

•   •   •

Hurrying along the hall in Police Headquarters, Cara turned into Hank Kelly's open doorway and stopped abruptly. There was a young man sitting in the chair across the desk from Hank.

"It's OK, Cara, Mr. Phillips was just leaving."

Phillips, most likely a student, Cara thought, gave her a friendly smile and passed by. She took the seat he'd left.

"Any luck?" she asked.

"Getting closer and closer to the moment, but no one who saw the snowman topple. It's like those astrophysicists getting closer to the moment of the 'Big Bang.'"

"How close?"

Hank was concentrating on tearing the wrapper off a Snickers bar. He held it out toward Cara.

"Want first bite?"

She took the candy, took a bite and handed it back.

Chewing, Hank answered, "Phillips there, was walking

along the Diag and passed by the snowman at 11:07. It was standing tall. He came back in the other direction at 11:14 and it was down."

"Seven minutes. How did he know the times so exactly?"

"He was meeting a friend at the corner of East and South University at 11:10 to borrow some notes. He was checking his watch, because he didn't want to be late. 11:14 is an estimate based on his own clocking of the distance this morning."

"What a thoughtful citizen," observed Cara. "He didn't see anything useful?"

"Maybe. Going, he observed nothing, but he admits that if someone were behind the snowman he probably wouldn't have noticed. He didn't stop. He'd seen the thing a little earlier when it was being built. Coming back in the other direction, however, he noticed two things: first, the snowman had fallen and second, he noticed a man walking in the same direction as he and about fifty yards ahead. Philips thinks he noticed him because the guy looked like a bum, and it was unusual to see such a person that deep into the interior of the university campus."

"Why a bum?"

"Right. Phillips had a hard time with that. He settled on the clothes and the mangy looking stocking cap. Also, when the guy turned the corner of North U and State, under the streetlight, Phillips got a quarter view of his face and had the impression the guy had a week's stubble."

Cara was following their steps in her mind's eye. "Phillips didn't go in the same direction at the corner?"

"No, he crossed State and took East William."

The partners stared into each other eyes as if an electrical connection were being made.

Cara's voice was challenging. "How could he not have seen Dennis Duke?"

"I had an idea about that. Picture this. Going from his hotel to the snowman, Duke had to walk in the same direction as Phillips did on his way to get his notes. What if Duke was walking behind Phillips a few yards—far enough back so the student wouldn't have heard his footsteps. Duke stopped to look at Mr. Snowman. Perp, who's hiding behind the snowman, used the vaulting pole to push the top half of snowman onto Duke, covering him and asphyxiating him. Phillips can't see this, because he has already passed through the Engineering Arch and turned right for several more yards to the corner where he met his friend. Perp was walking away as Phillips, returning through the Arch, starts walking along the Diag back toward State Street. Philips notices the fallen snowman and also the "bum" walking in front of him. 'Bum' equals killer. It's gotta be, because there's no other place for the killer to go except back toward State Street. If he'd gone in the other direction Phillips and his friend would have seen him coming out through the Engineering Arch."

"Nice thinking, Hank, only it leaves us now with the problem of identifying this 'bum.'"

"Yeah, I know."

"If Philips is right, the killer being a bum is welcome news to the university. I've just come from sitting in on a face-off between the university's council and the litigator Duke's business manager brought in. Combing aside the jargon, I

36

made it out that the school is liable only if Duke's death was accidental, which points to negligence on the U's part, or if he was murdered by a university employee in the act of performing some university designated duty."

"I get it," Hank replied. "The bum is not likely to be an employee, because while the U may not pay as well as long-distance trucking, it supports its staff better than 'bum' level."

"If you were a real pal, you'd let me have the last bite of the Snickers."

Hank made as if to give this suggestion long, serious thought, then started to hand it to her.

Cara leaned forward to take it as she said, "Here's the catch. If Dennis Duke was afraid to go outside alone at night, how could this 'bum' lure him to leave his hotel?"

"Good question," Hank replied and as if lost in thought over her question. At the same time, he put the last piece of the Snickers into his mouth.

.   .   .

Rebecca Bemis, secretary to I.B. Sames's agent, Henry Stockton, was looking up from an appointment calendar on her desk.

"You have I.B. scheduled for Ann Arbor in February. Hasn't the now apparent murder of Dennis Duke changed your thinking about that?"

"Not at all."

"Isn't I.B. concerned?"

"No. I told her there really had been no murder. The

whole business was a publicity stunt staged by the university and Duke to get more media attention for their award program and for Duke's next book, *The Undead,* which Duke, holed-up somewhere, is now busily finishing."

"Cool."

5

Andy Backus perched one buttock on the corner of Ruth Hackett's desk.

"I'm really surprised at you and Byron pooh poohing the notion that the murder is directly connected to Beasley's award nonsense."

"Really, Andy, I never classified you as a promulgator of conspiracy theories."

"I don't think you mean conspiracy, Ruth. It's paranoia you're attributing to me."

Ruth pushed up her lower lip with the eraser end of the pencil she was holding. "I take your point. You're saying the murder could not be a coincidence, and a paranoiac denies the possibility of coincidence. For them everything is related—related to themselves. You're right, you're paranoid."

"I'm relieved you agree. Now, where was I? Oh yes, I was asking you to consider the effect that a person's name has on his or her whole destiny. Freud said, 'Anatomy is destiny', I say, 'Name is destiny.' Could a child named Dracula have become anything but a vampire?"

Ruth played her part. "Impossible!"

"To get down to cases, take Alonzo Schlink. Could he have ever walked upright and straightforward? No. He was predestined . . ."

"Oh no." Ruth shook her head.

"Oh yes. He was predestined to SLINK."

Ruth smiled and thought to herself that Andy was right; Schlink did slink. She leaned back in her chair, torn between indulging in this pleasant banter with her friend and finishing the work on her desk.

She'd play a little longer. "But isn't it quite a jump from slinking to murdering?"

"Don't you see the psychology showing itself in the deed? The murderer hides behind the snowman. This is devious . . . sneaky."

"Ah, yes . . . slinking behavior. Officer, bring the handcuffs, we have our man."

"Not so quick. Would Schlink do anything without the other parts of his organism? Would Schlink slink his best without Sheets and Sleeves?"

"All three of them were behind the snowman?"

"Only in spirit. There was only room for one. Do you prefer Sheets for the job?"

Ruth was about to make a choice when she saw the trap. "Wait just a minute. I'm not joining your posse—not yet, anyway. But, I have to admit that you've got me leaning toward the perpetrator being a member of the English faculty. That narrows the field to about one hundred and fifty suspects, two hundred including graduate assistants. I suppose we could strike Henry Beasley from the list."

"Are you sure? This whole program could be his way of luring these authors here to dispose of them. Maybe his last service to literature before retirement."

Ruth laughed. "OK, two hundred suspects."

· · ·

Four weeks had passed since the discovery of Dennis Duke's frozen body. The next speaker in the series, I.B. Sames, was about to arrive on campus. The "derelict of the Diag" as he was known among the investigators, had not been identified. Opinion was mixed as to whether the police had to increase their vigilance during the campus visit of Ms. Sames.

Cara Bartoli, influenced by Andy Backus, decided to play it safe and station a couple of plain-clothes officers at the Bell Tower Hotel for the length of I.B.'s stay. The university security force would patrol the vicinity of the League Building where the lecture and dinner would be held. Ms. Sames's agent had been advised that it would be best if the author not leave her room unless in a detective's company or that of a designated delegate of the English Department.

Henry Beasley's excitement over the visit of the woman whose absolute power in the publishing world— rivaling that of the Sun King in his realm— was such that no one could get Henry's attention for any abstract subject like the safety of his guest.

The Friday of her visit was a typical, Midwest February night. The frigid ten-degree wind blowing in from the north packed a punch near zero. The English faculty, *en masse*, heads down against the buffeting wind, left their warm cars in the parking lot and, cursing Henry Beasley, dashed toward the shelter of the League. Harsh elements bring people together much as a war will do, there being a common source of external threat to assure the group that their own differences are puny. So the chatter was congenial as everyone found their preferred seats next to their friends.

"Have you ever read one of her books?" asked one.

"Goodness no. Mysteries?"

"As a matter of fact I did," said another. "Very strange experience. I was staying at my aunt's cottage last summer. My books were in my car and it was raining hard, so I looked around the cottage for something else to read. The only book in the entire place was a copy of Sames's latest novel. I began reading and soon I was fast asleep, dreaming I had been caught in a thicket. Sticking out from the twigs like thorns were copious, unnecessary and boring words that tore at my flesh as I rolled from side to side trying to escape."

Henry Beasley stood at the lectern adjusting the microphone up and down. A technician sprang forward and took it out of his hand and set it back in its original position.

"Speakers must first demonstrate their complete unfamiliarity with technology," growled Ruth Hackett. "It establishes that one is an intellectual."

Henry went through a glowing introduction that would have made Oscar Wilde blush, gave the mike one more adjustment and stood beaming as his elderly guest rose and made her way to the lectern. I.B. Sames looked down benevolently at the upturned faces and began to speak.

Byron Page was late—twenty minutes late. Outside the auditorium door, he paused and listened. The amplified voice he heard was unfamiliar. He carefully opened the door and looked in. The door opened into the side of the room, slightly behind the podium. I.B. Sames spoke in a sweet, droning voice, and displayed the same beatific, grande dame smile that adorned her book jackets.

Byron looked at the audience, intending to find where Andy was sitting. He was startled by what he saw. Every member of the English Department was fast asleep. It was as if a hypnotist had just snapped his fingers. He quietly closed the door and found a seat in the outside hall. To enter and take a seat among a room of sleeping people was daunting.

Eventually Byron heard Beasley's solo clapping, and soon afterward the doors to the lecture room opened and drowsy colleagues shuffled out and down the hall toward the dining room. Byron joined them.

Ruth Hackett signaled a waitress. "PLEASE. Could we have some strong coffee over here?"

"So, tell me about her talk," said Byron.

Ruth answered uncertainly. "It seems that her readers have been concerned about Inspector Dogleash's possible impotence. She was eager to deny the existence of the malady. She said that what with writing poetry and viewing corpses he had no time to do it properly."

Jack Sumner laughed out loud. "That wasn't it at all. She only wanted us to understand that his failure to get around to putting the question to his girl friend was because of his sensitive 'forbearance.'"

Paul Bonmot, who taught creative writing, took the chair next to Byron.

"Paul, you were there. What did you come away with on the impotence issue?"

"All I know is she minutely described all the furniture in Dogleash's London flat—so much furniture that there couldn't have been room to do it."

Byron looked from one to the other. "Yes, and then what?"

"She began by telling us what had formed her decision to become a writer," Ruth answered. "She had a second grade teacher who had the class lay their heads down on their desks while she read Walter Scott to them."

"No, it was Robert Louis Stevenson," interrupted Jack.

"She's a mystery writer—it must have been Poe," Paul decided.

Byron leaned back and surveyed the group. "I'm getting the impression that while her address might not have been memorable, it was very restful."

Jack Sumner looked up from his iceberg lettuce salad from which he had been trying to scrape a tenacious bile-yellow dressing, and considered Byron's summary. "Yes, I do feel rested."

At the end of the meal, Henry Beasley made the presentation of the plaque he himself had designed for his lecture series. I.B. Sames waved and blew a kiss to all present and left with Henry, who was escorting her back to the Bell Tower Hotel.

"Two down, four to go," commented a somber voice from the end of the table. It was Alonzo Schlink.

.   .   .

Byron made love to Cara in his bedroom on Thayer Street. Lying in the dark afterward he told her about the

Department's evening with Sames.

"Restful, eh?" Cara said. "Well, restful is what I want her whole visit to be. I've got a man sitting in the hotel lobby all night. He'll have breakfast at the table next to hers and see her off at the airport gate."

"It's pretty obvious you're really worried about something happening . . ." Sensing he was alone, he looked over and saw that she was fast asleep.

The next morning Cara came downstairs to Los Lobos's *La Pistola y El Corazon*. It was the accompaniment for the *huevos Mexicanos* Byron was whipping up: one of the four dishes for which the Viking stove was purchased. Cara poured herself coffee and settled in a chair that caught the thin February sun.

"We must go to Mexico sometime, so I can hone my recipe and technique," Byron said.

"OK, I can be ready this afternoon."

Byron began scooping eggs onto her plate. "I'd take you up on that, only I know you couldn't really enjoy yourself not having solved the case of the life-snuffing snowman."

"Maybe it's not a case at all," Cara said. "Maybe the snowman just toppled over by itself and the vaulting pole was wiped clean of fingerprints by a gloved sophomore making lewd gestures to a comely freshman."

"Who would have thought such a romantic image could have come out of such a crime-jaded head?"

"It's modern romance. Your problem, you don't keep abreast of the times. Evidence? You're not even pierced."

The phone rang. Byron answered and handed it to Cara. "Your man at the Bell Tower Hotel."

"Yeah, Tom." As she listened the flush of the pleasures of the night and morning drained away. "From where you were sitting you could keep an eye on both the elevators and the stairs? Yeah OK, I'll be there in five minutes." She hung up.

"Don't tell me I.B. Sames is missing," Byron joked.

"No, I'm afraid she's right where she's supposed to be—in her bed—but dead."

6

Cara stood at the foot of the bed. She felt herself an intruder, so peacefully asleep did Ms. Sames seem. Hank Kelly walked up beside Cara and broke the spell.

"Fell asleep reading one of her own books—figures."

"You mean that one of her books would put her to sleep?"

"No, I mean this crazy perp is jacking around with something that is known about the writer." Hank guessed Cara was wondering how he, who only read the prose on the back of wine labels, could know anything about the dead author's work. "My wife told me. 'Surer than Ambien,' she said."

The photographer was taking the last of her pictures. The digital chip registered a woman in her seventies, heavily made-up, eyes closed, sitting up in bed, pillows arranged at her back, wearing a bed-jacket, her hands holding a copy of her novel, *Death in an Awkward Position*. The bedside lamp was on.

The photographer finished and Cara, pulling on surgical gloves, moved forward and undid the closure of the jacket. Underneath it, she found that I.B. wore a slip. Cara went over to a dresser and opened the top drawer. There folded neatly was a silk negligee.

"What do you make of this, Hank?"

"The old dear traveled with two nighties."

"Wrong. That isn't a nightgown she's wearing under the bed jacket, but a slip. It means she didn't go to bed on her own. Not having removed that load of make-up is another clue. The killer opened this drawer, looked for a negligee, saw the bed-jacket and realized there was an easier way to create the image he wanted than wrestling her out of her slip and into a negligee—a nearly impossible task with rigor mortis setting in as it must have been in order for him to set her up in this pose. "

Cara contemplated the dead author again. "This is very sad, I'm sure many people loved her. She looks so peaceful, I doubt if any violence was involved. She must have been poisoned."

"Maybe *sleeping* pills," Hank offered.

Cara pointed her finger at him. "You got it. The autopsy will tell us."

She went to the corpse again and tried to move the hands that held the book.

"Rigor. I don't think there can be any doubt. This posing must have been done when the rigor was just forming—three or four hours after she died."

"Yeah, and her head wasn't flopping around. Almost as if he were modeling clay."

The two detectives went over the rest of the room thoroughly. Nothing of note was found except what wasn't found—sleeping medication.

Cara pondered the situation. "We'll have to know what substance was used in order to know when she ingested it. Some fast-acting substance like cyanide could have been given to her right here, but something like a barbiturate would have to have been put in her food at the dinner.

Cara picked up the phone on the bedside table and dialed the number for the university operator.

"This is Sergeant Bartoli of the Ann Arbor Police. Please connect me to the administrative office of the League."

Waiting, she took off the rubber gloves and laid them on the bed.

"Hi, this is Detective Bartoli of the Ann Arbor Police. I want to talk to the person who can tell me who did the catering for the English Department dinner held there last night. "

Cara wrote down a number, thanked the person at the League and dialed again.

"The University Catering Service," she said to Hank while she waited for someone to answer. She repeated her identity and told the person what she wanted.

"Oh, damn! Are you sure? Just came out of the machine . . . all of the dinner service? You're sure." She hung up, disappointment evident.

"The first thing they did this morning was wash the dishes from last night."

"How about the water jug and glass they provide for the speaker. Maybe that belongs to the League."

"Brilliant." She got the League, again, and asked the question. She put the phone down. "It's true, the water pitcher belongs to the League. They're going to find it and hold it for us."

"Good. Let's drive over there."

It was walking distance, but Hank never walked.

"Do you mind driving?" he added. "I haven't finished my Danish."

"The random-killer theory can be safely scratched, " Cara said, getting behind the wheel. "The English Department guests are the targets. We definitely need to talk to our department's psychological consultant. This perp is wacko."

"Yeah. Kinda fun, don'tcha think? Who's the next guest? Maybe we can figure out how the guy will be killed. But the problem is, the rest of the invited speakers will probably cancel and spoil all the fun."

"I'm worried about you. It's clear you're not getting enough job satisfaction. No doubt that's why you're eating too much."

"Eating too much? Have I gained weight?"

"No, and that might be another problem. You know—tapeworm."

"Oh, God. The cross I have to bear being your partner."

"Ask for another partner."

"Are you kidding? I already asked, and no one would trade with me."

They traveled the short distance to the League Building and parked in the "No Standing Zone" at the front entrance.

"This doesn't need both of us. Do you mind?" Hank said, licking his fingers.

•   •   •

Byron, impatient to get some information from Cara who'd left her uneaten eggs an hour earlier, walked out onto the sidewalk in front of his house. He stood there in his bathrobe, a tall, trim figure whose uncombed, blond hair was beginning to reflect a good bit of silver. It was a handsome face he turned toward the Bell Tower Hotel, marred only by a slightly deviant nose caused by a playground swing that a playmate had launched in his direction when he hadn't been looking.

Two police cars were parked down the block in front of the hotel in that negligent style favored by gendarmes the world over when called to a crime scene. Would they have parked that way if Sames had died of a heart attack? No way. He went back inside. It was cold and his feet were bare inside his slippers.

Back in the kitchen he glanced toward the answering machine. The light was flashing. Damn, she must have called while he was outside.

"Hi, it's me and it happened again. It looks like murder, probably an overdose of sleeping medication. We'll know later and I'll call you. Ciao."

Byron's thinking fast-forwarded past benign explanations for the two authors' deaths, and stopped at Andy's notion that a member of the English Department was the culprit. Next he remembered Alonzo Schlink's words, "Two down and four to go." But when could Schlink have . . . No point in speculating, he'd have to wait until Cara called again. In the meantime, he had to attend to the proofs of his book that must be corrected and sent back to his publisher. This insane author killing must be put out of mind so he could stay focused on the bigger event, the one the world waited for.

7

At that same moment, in the University President's house, which was directly across the campus from Byron's place, a familiar scene in this particular marriage was being repeated. A small, dark, middle-aged woman, as intrepid as a mongoose, faced the mirror in the master bedroom applying the final touches to her make-up while shifting her focus repeatedly to the image in the mirror of the placid, balding, rotund man who stood behind her. Listening to her, one would be reminded of a tiny, yapping Pekinese giving a docile Saint Bernard a piece of its mind.

"It's a long way up from President of Chestnut College to President of the University of Michigan. If you think for a moment I will agree to return to Chestnut Junction, Ohio, you're . . . well, I just won't let it happen—understand?"

"Yes, dearest." His clean-shaven face twitched and shock waves spread to his jowls.

"Your position here is as secure as the survival of the Arctic Tern. I don't have to remind you the vote was 4 to 3 when the Regents picked you last August as Interim President. Nothing must happen in these next months to make it easy for them to back down. Understand?"

"Yes, my dearest."

"The word is that one of the four who voted for you has already had second thoughts."

"Yes, dearest, so I've heard . . . from you."

"You and I know why they considered you in the first place. It was because your name is Lopez and it's politically correct at present to show respect for Latinos. Would we be here in this beautiful home right now if they realized an immigration officer in New York had misheard your grandfather say Lopeszch?"

In an effort to turn off the vituperative hosing, Felix Lopez spoke in a firm voice to the issue that had alarmed his wife.

"I have ordered Henry Beasley to appear before me this afternoon."

He thought about what he had just said and was pleased with his choice of words. Actually when he'd called Beasley he'd asked him to stop by the President's office sometime soon if he happened to be in the vicinity.

"I will not permit another of those lectures," Felix added, on a roll.

Evita Lopez thought the accurate statement should be, "We will not permit," but she let it go. He would need some self-confidence.

"Good, then you already told him."

"In a manner of speaking."

This made Evita pause, but Felix hurried to say, "You may go to your tea, knowing this problem has been resolved."

Evita, satisfied with both her cosmetic results and her swift handling of the potentially catastrophic problem of the murdered authors, picked up her purse.

Alone now before the mirror, Felix began trying out

various approaches he could use for the Beasley interview. The wise sympathetic leader: "I feel your disappointment, Professor Beasley. So much work invested . . . I'm certain you've given thought . . . " The decisive commander: "Cancel the program, Beasley! Tell the authors it's for their safety. Mail out the plaques." Collegially: "Between you and me Henry . . ."

The bedroom extension rang and Felix heard that Henry Beasley was waiting at that very moment in the President's office four blocks away at the Flemming Building. He bolted from the house, trotting while working at buttoning his overcoat.

Bursting out of breath into the waiting room of his own office, he found a smiling English Department Chairman.

"Oh, Beasley . . . that is Professor Beas . . . I mean to say, Henry. Please sit down, I mean, please come in my office and sit down."

Henry Beasley entered the office and chose a chair.

"This chair over here, I believe, is more com . . . but if you prefer. Or this one . . . "

Beasley eyed Felix Lopez like a lepidopterist waiting for a butterfly to alight.

Felix had forgotten to take off his overcoat, but since he seemed to have finally settled in his chair, Beasley thought it wise not to mention it.

Beasley took the initiative. "I'm so pleased you are recognizing the small contribution I and my department have made on behalf of the university. The series has enjoyed wide mention in the newspapers, as I'm sure you know."

Felix Lopez, open-mouthed, was experiencing acute distress.

In the absence of a comment, Henry further developed his appreciation of both his own program and his President's recognition thereof.

"Although a faculty is made up of mature scholars, at heart we are ever yearning for that word of encouragement from our leader. Mark my word, your esteem in our department will soar when I tell everyone of the generous support this meeting signifies."

Felix Lopez sat immobile for a good part of a minute. Some unbidden neurons deep in his temporal lobe caused his head to move slowly up and down. A profound nod.

Beasley would describe this deeply knowing nod to others all evening. Oh, the depth and wisdom of the man they had chosen for Interim President.

After the euphoric Henry Beasley left the office, Felix sat as puzzled at how all this had happened as one does after an encounter with a skilled shortchange artist.

While in this daze, a call came in from the head of the Buildings and Grounds Department to inform him that the university garbage collectors had gone on strike. Their two demands were, the union claimed, non-negotiable: first was a change of name from Waste Engineers to Divergent-Use Materials Specialists, the second was tenure.

"Tenure?" gasped Felix.

"Yeah, I kinda figured that would be tough for you academics to swallow, am I right?"

"Swallow?"

"I told the union steward he was outa his mind. He

started singing and I quote, 'Nobody knows the garbage you'll see.'"

"When will they go on strike?"

"They are."

"Are?" Felix felt as if he were Napoleon being told the British had broken through on both flanks and the center and a galloping sound was heard at the rear.

"This kind of garbage, the kind a university expels is paper and such, right? I mean, it doesn't smell, right?" asked Felix, hopefully.

"You wouldn't ask that if you'd smelled the sacrificed animals from the labs, or biological waste from the hospital, or . . . "

"No, don't go on. Please don't go on." Felix shuddered. "Tenure, you say?"

8

The Ann Arbor Police Department was fortunate that a moonlighting group of university chemists had set up a private forensic lab to supplement their academic paychecks. They specialized in speed and the unusual.

Hank Kelly sat on a stool eating a donut and watching the woman in the white lab coat work at a spectrometer.

"It's a benzodiazepine. Now, which one?" she said more to herself than to Hank, whom she'd mentally blocked out when he opened the bag of donuts and offered her one. "Odds are it's 7-chloro-1,3-dihydro-1-methyl-5-phenyl-2H-1,4-benzodiazepin-2-1, wouldn't you say?"

"Not when my mouth's full," Hank said around a mouthful of donut.

She swung around in her chair, smiling. "Or what your knowledgeable friends call diazepam."

Hank swallowed. "Yeah, right."

"Or, if they're at a cocktail party—Valium. I have to do some more work for a final identification, Hank, but this should tell you it was deliberate. Unless a person is bent on suicide, it's highly unlikely they could accidentally OD on benzodiazepine."

"Thanks, Frieda. Please call me as soon as you know the exact drug. We'll be able to start making pharmacy checks."

He got up and held out the open donut bag once again.

She glanced inside then gave him a cold stare. He looked into the bag half expecting to see that the bakery clerk had played a trick and included a toad. That would have surprised him, but not as much as someone turning down a glazed custard.

· · ·

Byron walked past Joan Arnold's desk.

"Oh, Professor Page. Did you hear about the letter Henry Beasley got from Michael O'Connell?" Joan called out.

"No," Byron replied.

"O'Connell was scheduled to be the fourth, best-selling mystery novelist to be honored. You knew that of course?"

"Roughly. What about it?"

"He cancelled. Said we had a crazy serial killer on our hands and while it's admittedly exciting, he wasn't going to contribute his own life to the fun."

"Good, his canceling shortens the hit list. He would have been here in April. It won't be the cruelest month *this* year."

"Not so. The first thing Henry did was to get the June honoree to move to April."

"Refresh my memory. No never mind. I'm sure he or she will cancel before April. Best-selling means—at the very least—survivor."

"Professor Page, I almost forgot, Detective Bartoli wants you to call her pager."

Byron went into his office and dialed Cara's pager. A few minutes later Cara called back.

"How's the investigation going, Sarge?" he asked brightly.

"You want me to tell you about the progress of my investigation?" she asked incredulously.

"Y-e-s," he replied, not understanding her attitude..

"You're very interested aren't you? Makes you curious about what will happen next?"

"Y-e-s."

"You would feel slighted if I kept the details from you?"

"Y-e-s."

"Well, how do you think I feel about your making me wait like everybody else to learn the identity of the real Shakespeare?"

"I don't believe it. I was prepared for standard police procedure—the rubber hose, cattle prods—but to attempt to make me feel guilty? I never dreamed you'd stoop so low."

"Ah, c'mon."

"I'd sooner die. The trust between an author and his or her publisher is as pure and sure as a baby's smile—unless it's suffering colic—the baby that is."

Byron could sense, however, that there was real irritation in her tone, so he added, "You know I want to tell you more than anyone, but as I suggested earlier, it would only be a burden to you to know and have to endure people quizzing you. I'm sure it has been much easier to just say, 'The creep won't tell me.'"

Cara didn't reply, so he prompted, "So, are there new developments in the case you can't wait to tell me about?"

Cara thawed. "Yeah, but somehow part of me says that

if you really loved me you wouldn't be able to help yourself; you'd have to tell me." She made an effort to lighten the moment. "Notice the difference between us. I have no choice, I'm just a love slave and I have to tell all. Yes, there is new information about the case. We now know what killed the lady—a lethal quantity of modern man's best friend, benzodiazepine."

"Any idea how it was given to her?" Byron said, glad to move into this topic.

"It must have been in one of the foods at the dinner. We checked the pitcher and glass from the speaker's stand. But, the *modus* remains a question mark and also how the killer gained entry into her room. She had strict instructions to open the door to no one. I think the perp came in only after the drug had taken effect. But, how did he get by the guard in the lobby and how did he get into her room? Any ideas? I've heard it said that Shakespeare covered all the topics, how about this one?"

"Hmm. Locked and unlocked. How about this:

'My purse my person, my extremest means

Lie all unlock'd to your occasion.' It's from *The Merchant of Venice.*"

"'Locked and unlocked', there's a thought. What if her door was never locked? What if the lock was tampered with? Gotta check something. Call you later."

Byron sat complacently and comfortably in his Harris tweed jacket gazing at the light snow blowing past his office window. No denying it, it was most pleasing to have a love slave. His thoughts went to what he'd just been told. Benzodiazepine. That would be Valium or one of its new cousins. Did he know anyone in the department who popped them? Not Andy or Ruth Hackett. Jack Sumner? He thought not. How about the "Three Musketeers"? Joan might know. And, of course, there was Leticia Grable. She taught "The Literature of Angst" and was reputed to down Valium like M&Ms. But she's as thin as a thought and shakes in the shade in August. There's no way she'd have stood waiting behind a snowman to waylay Dennis Duke.

He unlocked his filing cabinet and took out the proofs of *Please Let Me Introduce Mr. William Shakespeare.* He put the key in his pocket then stopped. The subject of locks brought a disturbing thought to his mind, the possible theft of the proofs. He had considered his withholding of the name of the writer of the plays as a dramatic lark—a literary teasing. Its effect had turned out to be stronger than he'd imagined, not only among Shakespearean scholars, but also with the public in general as well. The interest wasn't limited to English-speaking nations either; it was worldwide. A few days ago Maureen Dowd said in *The New York Times,* "The world has even forgotten about the price of oil, so engrossed has it become in the soon-to-be-solved mystery."

What would it be worth to a newspaper or magazine to beat the publication date—be first with the revelation? Plenty, Byron now realized. He walked over to the window and looked from his office in Angell Hall down onto State Street. That man there with his coat collar up and scarf wrapped around his face; was he looking up at Byron's window? He returned to the file cabinet and gave a locked drawer a yank. Between the face of the drawer and the cabinet frame was a space large enough to insert a screwdriver. Child's play for a professional, and the media would employ professionals. He would have to find some other place to keep the proofs until he finished working on them and returned them to Howard Forsyth at Cloistered Press. He'd even have to think of a way to send them back safely.

Now feeling compelled to keep the proofs safe, Byron crossed the hall to Joan's office, keeping an eye on his own office door.

"Joan, have you seen any suspicious characters hanging around the halls here, today?"

"Apart from the graduate students, you mean?"

A graduate student! What an ideal person for the media to employ—poor, undernourished, resentful for all the hoops we make them jump through!

"No, I mean *any* suspicious person."

"I'd have an easier time isolating the few who weren't suspicious. What are you concerned about, if I may ask?"

Of course, she was right. Everyone was suspect. Even Joan?

"Oh, nothing." He sidled out of her office and back into his own and shut the door.

He would have to take the proofs home with him when he finished working on them this evening. But, if he were being watched, this would be noted and his house might be burgled. And in the thief's single-minded fervor there was no telling the amount of damage that might be inflicted on his new woodwork, his antiques, even his Viking range. No, he mustn't carry anything home to arouse suspicion.

If not left in the file cabinet, then where? Perhaps he could put the proofs under some papers. No, everything in the room would be examined. Ah! It came to him. What better place to hide papers than in that colossal depository of miscellaneous paper—Andy's office. No one would find them there—certainly not Andy.

Byron crossed the hall again. "Joan, has Andy gone for the day?" Byron tried to give his voice an offhand note.

"Yes, I recall him saying, 'See you tomorrow.'"

"Would you give me the key to his office? I neglected to ask him for a book I need."

"Sure. Perhaps you'd like to borrow my ball of string."

"String?"

"I tie one end to the door knob when I have to go in there so I can find my way back out again."

Preoccupied and only half hearing, Byron mumbled, "String. Yes, the string."

"You all right, Dr. Page? You seem to be expecting trouble. You don't have an outstanding debt with a bookie, do you?"

"No, I guess it's all this fuss about the book. Has anyone been asking you questions about it?"

"What book is that? Only kidding. No one's asked me except my hairdresser, the supermarket cashier and my dermatologist—as he was dousing me with liquid nitrogen.

"Like the good secretary I am, I haven't bothered you with all of the details of the stir your book is causing. I get at least fifty calls a day. Beasley's secretary has decreed that all calls for the English Department not specifying Beasley personally are to be shunted onto my line.

"Most of the callers are civilized, but the rest." Joan

did the eye opening and eyebrow-lifting maneuver which the world reads as, "You'd be shocked to know." "Not very nice, indeed. You'd think that instead of revealing the authorship of some old plays, you had said you had proof the French don't know how to cook, or the Germans can't hold their beer, or the English upper lip is unusually flaccid."

"My God, it's as bad as that?"

Byron quickly retreated to his office and began working on the proofs until it was time to leave to meet Cara for dinner. He opened his door and looked down the long hallway. No one. He crossed the hall and unlocked Andy's door—back to his office to gather up the proofs—quickly back into Andy's cluttered room. Actually, the word "cluttered" depicted a condition far more organized than what he now viewed. Where in all this chaos could he trust his precious work? Over to the left he spotted a mound with the vague outline of a chair. This could serve as a landmark. He would deposit his proofs under the chair and stand a reasonable hope of finding them again.

This done, he opened the door a crack and checked the hallway. All clear. He locked the door and then headed toward his rendezvous with Cara telling himself his concerns were silly; still he felt great relief now that the manuscript was safely hidden..

"We got a couple of breaks," Cara announced as she was rolling the silverware out of her napkin. "One of them was courtesy of Mr. Shakespeare and Professor Page. But first I'll tell you about the drug that killed I.B. Sames. It wasn't Valium at all, but a rather uncommon one nowadays." She opened her notebook and read, "8-chloro-6-(o-chlorophenyl)-

1-methyl-4H-s-tria-zolo-[4,3]-[1,4]benzodiazepine."

"Did you say, 4-3 or 3-4?"

"4-3, of course. Triazolam or Halcion to those who have an aversion to numbers. It's a sleeping med that's no longer in fashion because of its reputation, deserved or not, of causing memory lapses. This makes it easier for us when we check with pharmacies. Ten years ago this wouldn't have been the case. Then it was sold by the bucket."

"Interesting. Deduction tells us we have a murderer who has not kept up with fashion, or one who has part of an old bucketful left over from the drug's glory days," reasoned Byron. "It seems to me I took Halcion once, but I can't remember."

"A tired joke, amigo. The other break is the one that you and Shakespeare contributed. It concerns the lock on I.B. Sames's door at the Bell Tower Hotel. The hole in the strike plate on the doorjamb into which the latch slides was filled in with something called Bondo. I'm told it's used for auto body repair and is quick drying. What happens is the door closes, but the latch can't slide into the hole in the striker plate and lock. Sames and I thought she was safely locked in for the night, but in reality the killer could walk in any time he liked."

"When he pushed the Bondo into the hole, did he leave a nice clear thumbprint?"

"Were life so easy."

"I remember using Bondo on an old jalopy of mine. Pink stuff."

"Makes one think. How many people would know about both Halcion and Bondo? That narrows the field. As a matter of fact y*ou* are the only person I know of, sir!"

"Now wait a minute, don't give me that look. Plenty of people would know," Byron exclaimed.

"Not me," replied Cara studying him with her dark brown eyes narrowed.

Byron waved the young waitress to their table.

"Excuse me, Miss," Byron said. "I'm sure you've heard of Bondo and Halcion haven't you?"

"Is that a comic strip?"

"Ah . . . possibly, but maybe you'd better bring us the wine list."

9

Byron had a duplicate key made to Andy's office before he went to work the next morning. His plan was to retrieve his proofs before Andy came in and return them to the confusion of Andy's litter each night until the work on the proofs was completed. He walked whistling into Joan Arnold's office and returned the borrowed key. When he was sure she was fully occupied, he used his new key to go in and gather up his proofs and quietly cross over to his own office door. He unlocked it and went inside. Immediately, he knew something was very wrong. When a man spends a quarter of his waking time in a room that has essentially remained the same for ten years, slight changes are as obvious as a seed between the teeth. There were many slight changes: desk drawers, office plants, bookshelves and his filing cabinet.

The file drawers were still locked and absent were scratches or other indications that they had been forced, but they had been opened and searched. The locks must have been picked—not much of a challenge to anyone knowing their trade.

His first impulse had been to immediately report the break-in; ask Joan to call the security office. He opened his door to do so. A former student passing by at that moment required a greeting, and this delay broke the flow of his intention. He backed into his doorway and reconsidered. A voice from the past, his father's, repeated a litany. "Measure twice, cut once." Byron had first heard it in the context of helping his father build a window box. But, his father explained, it was meant to apply to all of life's situations. Stop and think before you act, avoid a possibly irreversible error. "Once you've cut a piece of wood, you can't make it longer again," his father had said.

What were the consequences of reporting the burglary? The burglar had been careful to hide the fact of his search. He obviously didn't want to alert me, Byron thought. Is that just to avoid being hunted, or does it also mean he intends to try again? But if I conceal my knowledge that there has been a break-in, I then can become the misleader. I can lead him to believe I suspect nothing and that all of my actions are ingenuous, unguarded. The idea was appealing. He re-closed his office door.

Ten minutes later, he emerged, told Joan he had some errands to run, stopped down the hall at a colleague's office door for light badinage then left Angell Hall and bought a latte at Bruegger's before sauntering home. He walked out the front door of his home twenty minutes later carrying a box wrapped in brown paper and addressed prominently to his publisher with a black marker. This he carried to the UPS drop-off at Kinko's on Liberty Street and came out again, *sans* box, a few minutes later. He sauntered on to the Shaman Drum Bookstore where he browsed and bought a book of Jim Harrison's poems.

The box he had just handed over to UPS contained an early draft of the manuscript of an already published work on Shakespeare along with a cover note saying that this final draft of *Please Let Me Introduce* Mr. *William Shakespeare* was ready for publication. Byron planned to make a call—only a pay phone would be safe now—to Howard Forsythe, his editor, to explain the ruse. Should the burglar manage to intercept the box in transit and open it, Byron was counting on his knowing more about burgling than he did about Shakespeare.

• • •

The president of the local union was irritated and anxious. "You said they would knuckle under the first day. You guaranteed that the academics tender sensibilities could withstand long hours of pointless argument and meaningless harangue, but not one day of stench."

The union rep replied, "Yeah, I know. Problem is there's no stench. I'm told some fat dude wearing a cold-weather mask ran around all night picking up garbage and hauling it away in a Jeep Cherokee."

"Outa sight!"

"Yeah crazy, but that's what I heard."

"See what you can find out. Stench! We must have stench!"

• • •

A serious University President's lady appraised the University President across the breakfast table.

"You look like shit. Didn't you sleep last night? You would sleep better if you lost some weight."

"Yes, dearest."

"You have to be sharp today to deal with this ridiculous demand by the garbage men for tenure."

Felix Lopez was too tired to reply.

"By the way, forget your idea of canceling Beasley's visiting author program."

"But, wasn't that your . . . "

"I was talking to Cornelia Washtenaw at the tea yesterday. She's the wife of the university's legal councilor, and she says her husband is afraid if the series is canceled it will be viewed as the school's admission that the authors were killed because they were participating in a university-sponsored activity. He says the school must take the position that it is only a coincidence they were killed immediately after being honored."

Evita was constantly prodding him to be more forceful, so he said with spirit, "Only a fool would buy that. The series must be canceled. Who cares what this . . . this Washtenaw guy . . . "

"Cornelius. Cornelius Washtenaw."

"And his wife's name is, Cornelia?" pondered Felix.

"Her brother is one of the Regents who voted for you . . . the one who is having a change of heart."

An exhausted President Lopez heard this with ambivalence. He hated kowtowing to the regents, but he was relieved to know he wouldn't have to confront Beasley again. The man wouldn't listen.

"So, the series must go forward," she said with an emphatic gesture.

"Yes, dearest."

．　　．　　．

At five in the afternoon of the next day, there was a rap on Byron's door at the same time that it was being opened—Andy's usual procedure. Byron didn't know why Andy bothered to knock. Maybe if one were picking one's nose there'd be time to turn it into a scratch. Andy held a shielding hand above his eyes like an Indian scout and made as if he were trying to read—up side down—the page of manuscript Byron was working on.

"C . . . h . . . r . . . i . . . s Christopher Marlowe! Just as I guessed."

"Are you sure?"

Andy went through the charade again. "Oh no, it's F . . . r . . . a . . . n Francis Bacon!"

"Very good, only this happens to be Ruth Hackett's paper on the unconscious meaning of money in the novels of Jane Austen."

"It was a gamble. I'm outa here. You about finished?"

"I'll be a while yet."

"See you tomorrow." Andy zipped up his down parka and closed the door behind him. The sound of his steps receded in the hall.

Byron had only been waiting for Andy to leave so he could re-deposit the proofs in Andy's office. Byron picked up the pile of proof sheets and opened the door and again peered each way down the hall. All clear. Across the hall, key in the lock, in the door and close it. Safe.

He carefully picked his way through the stacks of books and papers, afraid that if he nudged one of them he'd be buried in the avalanche. The heap over in the corner, which represented the chair, was his destination. He bent over and was sliding his bundle under the chair when he noticed a box that was shoved farther back against the wall. Byron pulled it out and took off the lid. He was looking at the title page of a manuscript of *Breach of Confidence*, by Andrew Backus.

Byron lifted this page and read the next. "Chapter 1." The first paragraph began, "I'd make up some excuse to get him to an isolated place—open a couple of beers—offhand I'd say, 'I understand you're screwing my wife.'" A good opening sentence.

What a surprise, Andy had written a novel. He'd never mentioned any interest in writing fiction. In fact, he'd even *denied* any interest. This was too good. Byron had to read more of it—just a little, then put it back and leave.

It was ten o'clock when Byron turned off Andy's desk light. He hadn't been able to put the book down. It was a mystery novel with a clever plot about a psychiatrist whose patient told him how he was going to murder his wife's lover. It was well written; that went without saying. It moved swiftly and easily and the characters were well drawn. Byron ended up really liking some of them and was disturbed by the villain. Andy had written a damn good read.

So the old boy has it in him. The more surprising discovery was that Andy had not intended to hide his light under a bushel. He'd sent it to several publishers and had received their rejections. The letters were all saved at the bottom of the box, ten of them. Byron read these too. "Not for our list." "Mystery not strong enough, but well written." "Uneven writing, but mystery strong." "Good pace, but

characters weak." "Strong characters, but pace not sustained."
They were wrong. All wrong.

Byron was wistful as he walked slowly home on this
early March evening. The day bore the awakening message
of spring—that indescribable something in the air that
seemed to promise man one more chance to get it right.
Discovering Andy's novel had caused him to feel upbeat. His
friend hadn't been stagnating as he often claimed. Byron
wondered now what he should say to Andy. He felt strongly
that he wanted to give his friend a "five," punch him on the
shoulder. "That was great man! Don't give up on finding a
publisher." But, at the same time he knew that Andy had
kept it a secret. He'd also have to explain that he'd had a
duplicate key made to Andy's office. He decided he'd wait—
he'd "measure twice"—give it more thought.

10

A month had passed since the demise of I.B. Sames and once again the entire English faculty and more than a few uninvited, morbidly curious faculty members from other departments filled the auditorium of the Michigan League Building.

Hamilton Bede, the noted Middle-English scholar, whose renown rested upon his discovery, gained through a study of comparative spelling, that Chaucer had spoken with a lisp, sarcastically inquired of his neighbor, "And whom are we celebrating this evening?"

"Yet another 'much praised but-not-altogether-satisfactory lady'," answered Jack Sumner.

"And by what name shall she be praised?"

"Lou Saffron."

"Isn't she the abecedarian?" put in Ruth Hackett.

"Yes, and she is all the way up to 'W,'" answered Andy Backus. "We have but three more letters to endure."

"Mercifully, God in his infinite wisdom limited the alphabet to twenty-six letters. *Dabit deus his quoque finem*," returned the Bede.

"Not to worry," said Ruth. "She is laying down her pen after her next novel. A student of mine, who would willingly take up that pen, tells me Saffron is so rich she has just bought Santa Barbara's Municipal Pier and is putting all of her time into converting it into a villa."

"Maybe she'll retire sooner than that," Alonzo Schlink was heard to mumble.

The hubbub abated. Henry Beasley led a pleasant looking, shy, sixtyish woman to a seat on the podium; his manner was solicitous in a way *Mrs.* Beasley could only vaguely remember.

During the usual fussing over water and microphones a whispered commentary resumed throughout the audience.

"I understand she was afraid of coming here and wanted to cancel, but her publisher wouldn't hear of it. After O'Connell cancelled, her handlers believed it vital to the reputation of female detectives that she appear here brave and tall."

"She doesn't appear very brave tonight. She looks about the same way I would if I were in her shoes," said Ruth Hackett. "I'll bet she wishes she'd retired after *V is for Valkyrie.*"

Beasley was now ready for the introduction and looked out smilingly over the packed auditorium. Without waiting for the crowd to become quiet, he began.

"Our third guest in this series needs no introduction here or anywhere," he began. "In a recent survey of Americans age fifteen and older, more respondents could identify Lou Saffron than Edgar Allen Poe, Arthur Conan Doyle, Dorothy L. Sayers, Georges Simenon, and Dashiell Hammett combined. I think that settles any doubt that she and our other invited guests stand at the head of the mystery novel genre. It places them at the high water mark of literary achievement, because judged by the most reliable standard of all—the amount of money people are actually willing to spend—the mystery novel is king."

Beasley paused here as if to say he would invite anyone disputing this to step outside to settle it in a manly way. There was no challenge. Beasley relaxed and continued.

"I know you are, as I am, eagerly awaiting the words Ms. Saffron has prepared for us. Please welcome Lou Saffron."

The applause was decent, no doubt out of courtesy and encouragement to the woman who edged hesitantly forward to the microphone. Here, she seemed to try to get as much of herself as possible behind the shelter of the speaker's stand while she anxiously searched the audience for a potential assassin.

"Thank you very much, Dr. Beasley. Your introduction is much too generous. My presentation this evening is brief."

In a loud whisper, someone said, "Doesn't want to be a standing target for long."

Lou Saffron reached for the water glass, thought better of it, cleared her throat and began.

"My presentation is titled, 'The ABCs of Pleasure.'"

She took one more quick survey of the audience then began.

"Any Bavarian can deliver encomiums for great hasenpfeffer.

In Japan, kotos lax maidens' notions of pastimes.

Quarrels regularly succumb to Umbrians' very warm, xanthus, yummy zabaglione."

She smiled and said, "Thank you," then walked back to her seat.

"What the hell was that?" murmured Byron.

There was a general rumbling throughout the

auditorium where similar reactions were being voiced. Beasley looked thunder struck.

Suddenly Jack Sumner leapt to his feet shouting, "Brava! Brava! Brilliant! Scintillating! Coruscating!"

Everyone was agape. Complete silence.

"Don't you see?" exclaimed Sumner facing around toward his stunned colleagues. "She has run the alphabet!"

Again a rumble ran through the crowd.

"So she has," allowed Andy. "And, so she has." He got to his feet with all the others and joined in applause.

The dinner afterward was a happy affair. Everyone was in a good mood. Conversation flowed. Almost no one noticed that Lou Saffron pushed her food around on her plate but never took a bite.

Outside the building a balding fat man was searching through the bushes that lay along the route Lou Saffron and her entourage would take to the Bell Tower Hotel. Satisfied there was no hidden attacker, he retreated across South University to take up a position from which he could keep an eye on the rooftops of campus buildings along the way.

When Lou Saffron with her escorting group arrived at the hotel, Cara Bartoli, Hank Kelly and four officers in plain clothes met them. Lou Saffron's room had been searched minutely. Water analyzed by the police lab was provided for her to drink and wash. The ventilating system had been turned off and an electric heater was provided for the night. An officer was stationed at the top of each of the stairwells. The identification of the other hotel guests was checked and photos were taken of them when they registered. (Three couples about to register declined to have their pictures taken and quickly retreated from the building.) Cara stayed with Lou Saffron until she had completed her evening toilette. Cara lowered the shades, turned off the light and locked Lou Saffron in her room.

Cara stayed at the hotel until she was sure all was quiet and was about to sneak off to Byron's where he'd promised to make a midnight snack, when the detective whom she'd assigned to stakeout Alonzo Schlink's house called her. His cruiser was parked at the end of the dark Stratford Court cul-de-sac in a position to watch both Schlink's front and side door.

"Our man just came out the side door of his house dressed in black and walked toward the rear."

Cara had ordered the stakeout because she had come to take seriously the threats Schlink and the two other musketeers had made and especially so the comment Byron had overheard, "Two down and four to go."

Cara told the detective she would be there in a few minutes. She went over to Hank Kelly who was at a table in the lobby, eating a soft pretzel and studying his poker hand.

"Schlink is afoot. I'm going to go take a look."

"I hope you've got your long underwear on. it's cold out there, Sarg."

The detective who'd called Cara was standing on the walk in front of Schlink's house when she, with headlights off, came to a stop. He quickly led her down the side of the house and into the back yard. Here the lot fell away sharply to the next street. They heard a dog bark below them on Vinewood Boulevard. Down the hill they ran in pursuit.

Gaining the sidewalk, they saw a black figure pass through the yellow circle thrown by the corner streetlight.

Cara and the other detective crossed to the opposite side of the street and followed. It was difficult to see their quarry against the dark background. They hurried along as quietly as possible. Then, for an instant, they saw the interior light go on in a parked car half a block ahead, heard a door slam, then the chirp of tires as the car accelerated away. A block farther along, the headlights were turned on.

"That's him!" Cara exclaimed.

"Yeah, I'm afraid so."

Cara pulled out her cell phone and got the dispatcher to alert the mobile units to be on the lookout for a dark-colored car. She didn't even know the make or model.

The two returned to sit in Cara's car, heater turned on max, hoping to hear that one of the cruising police cars had spotted the car. No luck.

"Was Schlink the driver, or was someone waiting for him? What do you think?

He was a passenger. I didn't hear the car start up. The driver must have been waiting with the engine running."

"I think you're right—to keep warm just like us. I'm going back to the hotel. You stay here and watch for his return. Take him in for questioning."

Her news, when she got back to the hotel, broke up the poker game. The need for vigilance took over. There was no way they were going to let anyone get past them.

At two o'clock, the detective called in to say Schlink had returned by the same route he'd left. The detective had apprehended him and was holding him in the back seat of his patrol car. Schlink had refused to say anything about where he had been and was demanding that his attorney be called.

"Hold on a moment, Sam," Cara said. She needed time to think. Nothing had happened here at the hotel in the two hours Schlink had been out of his house. It was impossible for him to have entered the hotel. Wherever he had been, it hadn't involved Lou Saffron. Taking him to the station might result in nothing but trouble. She made up her mind.

"We'd better let him go, Sam. Feces may be fanned if we don't."

"You're sure?"

"Yeah."

Her beeper beeped while she was talking. She looked at the display. Byron's number.

"Hi, beautiful," he said. "I know you must be hungry and the night chef is here and ready to meet your every desire . . . as long as it's Welsh rabbit."

Cara had been too occupied with business to consider the state of her hunger, but now she discovered Byron was right—she was famished. She told Byron she was on her way and informed Hank Kelly where he could reach her.

The aroma of Welsh rabbit greeted her at Byron's front door. This dish was another of the four that required the Viking.

"Done in a jiffy. Have a seat and relax," he said stirring in some mustard.

There was a small sitting room off the kitchen. She flopped in a deep easy chair and began relating the hound and hare adventure with Alonzo Schlink. At the same time she idly turned the pages of a back issue of Architectural Digest.

"Hey, Byron," she called through the archway to the kitchen. "Have you seen this issue of Architectural Digest?"

"No, I haven't. I haven't had time to look at the last few issues."

"Guess whose house is in here. Lou Saffron's—her new villa on the pier."

"No kidding."

Byron went on with his preparations and Cara read the article.

"Get this, the architect is having to design a special screened enclosure over her swimming pool because of her allergy to bee sting. She says she has to protect herself all the time. 'I prefer to take vacations in the winter to climates where there won't be any bees to worry about.' How about that?"

"Well, she certainly came to the right place," Byron commented, pouring the golden lava of cheese onto two plates.

Cara gasped. "Oh, my God, I never prepared for something like bees."

"You're kidding. I just said Ann Arbor in March is the safest place she could be."

"Just the same, I'm going to run over to the hotel."

"The rabbit is ready."

"I'll be right back." She was out the door and running down the block without her coat.

"Bees? Gimme a break, Cara." Hank Kelly had gone back to playing cards with two of the other detectives.

Cara went over to the desk clerk. "Ring Lou Saffron's room for me."

He did so and there was no answer.

"She's just afraid to answer," offered Hank.

"Come with me." Cara said to the clerk. "And bring

your pass key."

There was no response when Cara knocked on Saffron's door. "Open the door," she said to the desk clerk.

The man did so and Cara charged in and turned on the light.

Lou Saffron lay on the floor white as milk. Her eyes stared at the ceiling, her expression desperate as if she had died struggling. She clutched a white and yellow cardboard box. "EpiPen" was printed on its side.

Hank had joined Cara now.

She knelt down and read, "epinephrine auto-injector."

"She was trying to get to her emergency adrenaline, but . . . " She brought her eye to the level of the opening of the box. "It's still in the box . . . she didn't make it. Poor lady!"

They both heard a buzzing sound and looked up together.

"Was that a bee that flew out of the room?" Hank exclaimed.

He ran into the hall, but it was gone. He returned to the room where Cara was examining the side of Lou Saffron's neck.

"Look here, Hank. Get a load of that swelling."

The right side of the author's neck was swollen twice the size of the left, the bright red skin contrasting with her general pallor. At the swelling's center a small, pale circle stood out.

"That's the site of the sting. She almost saved herself. The killer must not have known she'd carry adrenaline with her."

"That is, if it was murder," Hank said. "How could anyone get into this room? As strange as it would be, maybe the bee was already in the room . . . a dormant bee left over from last summer. Maybe it was a spider. She could also have been allergic to spiders. Don't you think it's likely you're jumping to the conclusion that this is another murder because you're expecting one?"

Cara stared at Hank ready to argue, but hesitated. He did have a point.

It was only then that both she and Hank let themselves look at the remainder of the room. Simultaneously, they glanced at a table near the window. Their eyes were drawn to a word written on it in bright yellow chalk. There could no longer be doubt that Lou Saffron had been murdered.

11

Cara entered the back entrance to Police Headquarters, while Hank sought the automobile fleet maintenance officer to report a problem with their cruiser's steering.

Sturges, the detective on the duty-desk, motioned to Cara.

"Kimble wants to see you, Cara."

She gave a knowing nod. Glen Kimble was the Chief of Detectives. It was known he had an ulcer and it was sure to be bleeding this morning. Kimble hadn't interfered with their investigation so far, but three murders with no suspects? No chief could cut you that much slack.

She went into the office she shared with Sandy Dorsey to hang up her coat. The secretary had put a message on her desk. "Call Jocelyn Jackson at her office."

Cara hadn't seen her housemate in several days. It could probably wait, but then she just might be so roughed up by Kimble that she'd forget to call. She dialed Jocelyn's, number at the Keen Arena.

"Jocelyn Jackson speaking."

"It's me, Jocie."

"Oh, Cara." The professional control left her voice and anguish took its place. "It's my niece, Willie. She ran away from home. At least that's what we think. She didn't come home last night."

"Is there a problem—I mean at home—I mean more than usual?"

A tense relationship prevailed between Willhemina Droost and her mother, Jane, Jocie's older sister. Willie was fourteen, precocious, volatile, and afflicted with that clear insight that most of us have for a short time before it is lost in the sandstorm of practical survival: the adult world is false and hypocritical. Hers was a virulent case.

Her father Doctor Jacob Droost was an Associate Professor of Neurosurgery who watched the struggle between the two women in his life from a distance, a position dictated both by his temperament and the real demands of his profession.

"Jane thought she smelled marijuana smoke in Willie's room and questioned her about it. Boom! And, there's more."

There always is, thought Cara. "And, Jane has checked with Willie's friends?"

"Yes, Cara, we did all that. I wouldn't call you knowing the stress you're under if we hadn't."

Here was a problem. The case should be given over to the Family Division of the Detective Bureau, but Jocelyn was her best friend and Cara knew the family was looking to her personally for help.

"My chief wants to talk to me right now, but I'll call you back. OK?"

"Thanks Cara. I'll be here in my office."

"Come in Cara, have a seat. Fill me in on Lou Saffron." The Chief of Detective's voice contained both an offer of continued friendship and a threat of the end of the same.

"We definitely have a psycho on our hands, Chief. It's obvious the targets are the bestselling mystery writers invited here by the English Department. So far we haven't much. Damn little. Here's what we have. The only lead in the Dennis Duke murder is that close to the time of the murder a student spotted a person on the Diag who appeared to be a vagrant. Inquiry through our usual contacts in that community has failed to produce any results. Second murder: A fatal dose of a sleeping medication called Halcion was probably introduced into something the writer ate at the dinner in her honor. Also, her room was entered in spite of the fact Hank and I had men stationed in the lobby watching the stairs and the elevator."

"I hear ya tellin' me this is someone with knowledge of the workings of the English Department and also knowledge of the setup in the hotel. How do you think he got into the room?"

"Like you said, he had to be familiar with the place to know the room I.B. Sames was in. He filled the strike plate hole with Bondo, so the latch couldn't slide home. Her door, in other words, was never locked."

"So, the guy came in by some back way and went upstairs to an open door. No prints, I take it?"

"Right. The killer then proceeded to have fun setting up the scene to look like she fell asleep reading. The theory that's rife among the English faculty is that these writers are being killed in a way that relates to their novels. The Duke guy writes about weird, supernatural, evil forces. A snowman crushes him. Apparently I.B. Sames has been writing some pretty boring novels of late, so the killer propped up her body to look like she was reading one of her own novels and it bored her to death. Last night the perp knew the novelist was hugely allergic to bee sting and managed to get a bee or bees into her room. When she was stung, she made a desperate effort to inject herself with adrenaline she carries for emergencies, but died before she could manage it."

"Jesus." Kimble registered revulsion. "And, I take it you put this lady to bed, tucked her in and made sure the door was locked this time."

"Exactly. We also screened the other hotel guests—all academics from other institutions here on business. None had been registered at the time of the other two murders."

"If you're sure the door was locked, how did the murderer get in the room?"

"I don't know. Maybe he picked the lock."

"Couldn't the bee have been put in the room earlier, while she was at the dinner?"

"Possibly," Cara agreed, "I might not have been aware of a single bee in the room before I left her for the night. But I looked around the room carefully and I would have seen the message he left for us."

"Message?"

"Yes, he wrote across the top of a table in bright yellow chalk in letters a foot high the word "SEE" with an arrow pointing to a dead bee that was lying on the table. He wanted to make sure we understood how she'd died."

Glen Kimble thought for a moment. "Was this babe some kinda of nature writer? I mean, how do the bees figure in her writing?"

"I don't know . . . yet."

Kimble thought again. "Are there more of these lectures?"

"Two more, in April and May. There were to have been seven, but three have cancelled. The man originally scheduled for April canceled first. He just said, 'You've got a nut running loose—count me out.' The writer scheduled for June . . . ah, Tony Quiverman, said he had to stay on the Navaho reservation to attend a sweat."

"A sweat?"

"I could be wrong. Another one, James Lee Burp claimed he had to remain in Louisiana to help a friend make sorghum molasses."

"Sorghum molasses?"

Cara shrugged.

"But, you say there are two more?"

"That's right. A guy who is very macho and refuses to flinch and a woman who believes her life is charmed."

"Damn it all, what's wrong with the university that it doesn't call a halt to this stupid business?"

"As I hear it, the legal advisors are afraid canceling could be read as an admission the murders were related to the lectures and would therefore support libel suits. The three victims earned big bucks. Their dependents might easily claim the authors' untimely deaths deprived them of . . . well, fortunes."

"The university has insurance."

"Yes, but donors don't consider that. They read the U is paying out multi-bucks on law-suits and they think, 'I don't want my contribution going to pay for somebody's stupid mistake.'"

Kimble changed his tone. "Cara, I don't want you to take this the wrong way."

Here it comes, she thought.

"Cara, I know you an' Hank been doin' your best, but I can't tell ya how many phone calls the boss has had, from the Governor's Office, from Mystery Writers of America an' what all. Understand, I'm not taking the case away from the two of you, but I've got to do something to . . . well you know the way it is."

Kimble looked into Cara's stony gaze and knew she wasn't going to help him any.

"What I've decided to do is ask the FBI for assistance from their Behavioral Sciences Unit, the ones who do suspect profiling on serial crimes. I want them to help you and Hank by doing one of them profiles for you. What you think?" He smiled and looked at her hopefully.

Cara relaxed. "Yes, Chief I think it's a great idea. When will they have time to look at our data?"

Kimble's eyes did some involuntary twitching "Well, actually they flew in this morning.

"Really? They?"

"Two of 'em."

"Where are they?"

"In the conference room looking over your reports."

"I see, and what did you think of them?"

Kimble's eyes went into something the docs call oculogyric crisis. He didn't seem to notice that Cara got up and left the room.

She walked down the hall to the office of a rookie detective to whom she had given the task of scanning the area pharmacies for Halcion prescriptions.

"Hi, Sergeant," the young man said eagerly. He didn't know if it would be appropriate to ask about the new murder or just deliver his report. He played it safe.

"I have the information for the whole county. I was waiting for Rite Aid's data. It took them a while to search their system."

He held out a manila folder to Cara.

"Thanks, Ted. Anything stand out?"

"Like you expected, the drug isn't used much anymore. A few patients who began using it back some years ago have continued and a few doctors seem to keep prescribing it. There is one person who fits the first group who is on the list you gave me of the English faculty, a Dr. Alonzo Schlink."

"Schlink? Well, well. When did he get his last refill?"

"Here's the best part. He got thirty pills last August and none until February third, when he got thirty more."

"Just ten days before I.B Sames came to town. Very interesting. Thanks, again, Ted."

Cara returned to her office and called Jocelyn Jackson and arranged to meet her at Jocie's office in an hour. She took a deep breath and started toward the conference room on the second floor. Passing the women's restroom, she made a quick turn. Better be relaxed. Better comb her hair. Better to be cool and under control.

The two FBI agents looked up when she entered the room with a superior, 'who might you be' expression. One was about thirty and cocky. The other was maybe fifteen years older, and very much the one in charge—the cock-of-the-walk—except she was female.

"Hi, I'm Sergeant Bartoli, my partner Hank Kelly and I are working the three murders."

The woman feigned misunderstanding. "Working? Did you say working?"

Cara didn't answer. The woman's barb had been delivered beautifully, subtly. One couldn't prove whether it was an insult or that she hadn't heard Cara clearly. The woman was a splendid actress. Cara was reminded of Charlotte Rampling. She did look like her, except her hair was black, sleek and smoothed tight to her face.

"We've been looking over your evidence. You haven't got diddly, have you?" The young guy said it, and Cara knew he wouldn't have had the nerve unless he was sure of his partner's approval.

"I seem to have missed something. Have we been introduced?" Cara asked coolly. It was a good thing she'd stopped at the john.

"Excuse me, Sergeant. I'm Special Agent Twyla Mann and this is Special Agent Bunce Bradford."

Cara pulled out a chair, sat, looked fixedly at Bradford and said, "Would you quantify 'diddly' for me?"

Agent Mann silently marked one up for Cara. Bradford blushed. Cara thought, "Bunny" Bradford. Yes, that's what he would have been called at Choate. She could handle him. She wasn't so sure of the Dragon Lady.

The woman spoke. "I think Agent Bradford is impressed that the murders must have been committed very skillfully, since there was so little evidence collected."

"Oh, is that what he meant? Well, that happens to be the case, at least not the kind of evidence that lends itself to investigation. Take last night, there were no prints and no suspicious fibers found in the room. The only thing left behind was a bee, a honeybee and a chalked message. You see, the killer used a bee as the murder weapon. He left the bee, or at least *a* bee on the table in the victim's room and an arrow pointing to it. We are planning to do a thorough search for the source of that bee. I have an appointment with an entomologist at the university, but I have a hunch it's going to be difficult to put the killer and the bee together."

This sharing of information had failed to generate a thawing temperature as Cara had hoped. It was clear she was to know she was with her superiors.

"You have consulted the Violent Criminal Apprehension Program data base?"

Cara was loath to answer, but she might as well and get it over with and be about her business. These dudes were here and that was that.

"Yes, of course."

Agent Mann quite clearly hadn't expected this answer. She turned a page of the file on the desk. "We will be examining the details of the cases as well as the lives of the victims in order to formulate our profile—it will be accurate. Possessing this profile, the task of matching it to the possible suspects should be a simple matter."

Cara had an impulse to say, "Are you real?" but she didn't.

"When do you expect this . . . er . . . profile to be completed?"

"Sooner than you think," answered Twyla Mann, pleased to see that she had gotten to Cara. "Some things are obvious immediately. First, the murderer desperately wants to get attention. Actually, you need do nothing but wait and ignore this person and he or she will have to advertise more blatantly and carelessly. That, of course, would entail more murders, so we are forced to abandon that strategy."

"Pity."

"Secondly, these are highly theatrical productions—histrionic, wouldn't you say?"

"On the tip of my tongue."

Special Agent Twyla Mann smiled knowingly. She deduced the local-yokel detective needed to resort to defensive sarcasm.

"We'll call you when our work is complete." She dismissed Cara by beginning to converse with her young partner in low tones.

Cara was angry. She got up and left the room without another word and closed the door slowly to keep from doing the thing she really wanted to do. She must remain focused on the work in progress. The autopsy was being performed at that moment and she wanted to be sure the lethal agent was the bee venom and not some other substance injected by the killer. She would talk to the pathologist, but first she'd drive to Keen Arena and talk to Jocie. Hank was in his office and agreed to meet her at the morgue in an hour.

Opening the car door Cara paused. The attitude of the two FBI agents had affected her in spite of her attempt to dismiss it. Hell, they were right. Here were three flamboyant murders. The killer was practically thumbing his nose at her and what did she have? One member of the English Department had been heard saying that Lou Saffron might retire sooner than she expected to. The same guy had refilled a drug he'd been taking for years and the whereabouts of him and his two buddies was unaccounted for during the time of Saffron's murder. She brightened. Maybe she had more than she'd credited.

12

"What did Willie take with her when she left?" Cara asked.

"We think she took her backpack—at least we can't find it. Maybe a few pieces of clothing. A sweatshirt is missing."

"She didn't pack as if she were planning to be away a long time," Cara deduced.

"That's what's worrying us so. If she were angry and wanted to teach Jane a lesson by running away for a few days, wouldn't she take a few more of her clothes? And she didn't have any money. She'd just spent her savings on a mountain bike, which is still in the garage. We're afraid she's been abducted."

"But didn't she leave right after this blowup with Jane?"

"Right. It's so confusing."

"I see that it is." Cara watched the anxiety play over her friend's familiar features. "I think I know Willie pretty well. I feel strongly that her disappearance has to do with her and Jane. And the fact she hasn't taken much with her means she hasn't gone far. I'll file a missing person's report anyway and put out an APB with her description."

"Oh, I hope you're right. Thanks, Cara."

"Jocie, remember Willie is not a child. And although she's only fourteen, I know of few adults who are better able to take care of themselves."

"Oh, I know, I know," Jocie said and hugged Cara, wetting Cara's cheek with her tears.

• • •

Cara gripped the cold handle of the autopsy room door and with dread, pulled it open, took two steps inside and stopped. The autopsy was still in progress. Hank stood watching and gave Cara a nod. Cara couldn't get used to autopsies; they seemed like such a violation, such an indignity. This seeming disrespect for another person bothered her more than the sight of internal organs.

Lou Saffron's scalp had been pulled down over the top half of her face like a sock pulled down over a shoe. This was done in order to saw open the skull and remove the brain. Once removed, sliced and examined, it could be returned to the vault of the cranium and the scalp pulled back in place giving the appearance that nothing had been done. The "diener", or assistant, was occupied with "running the bowel." This involved slicing the intestines open longitudinally with scissors. The odor was what you'd expect.

Hank was chewing beef jerky.

"Good morning, Cara. It is still morning I hope," said Dr. Burgess, the County Medical Examiner, glancing at his watch. "I've got a lot of work to get through today."

"Sorry to burden you again so soon with our stiffs," returned Hank.

"Yes, I'd appreciate it if you'd solve these murders soon."

"Everybody's in a hurry nowadays," said Hank.

"I'm not through, but I'm pretty sure I won't find anything more of note. She died of anaphylactic shock. He held out a kidney he had sliced in half. "See how pale."

Burgess then pulled Lou Saffron's hair away from the side of her neck. An elliptical cut had been made at the point where Cara had originally seen the pale center of the huge swelling.

"Quite a reaction," commented Burgess. "I've taken a tissue sample of the area where the insect's stinger penetrated. I'm sending it to a colleague at UCLA Medical Center. I've a hunch this is a killer bee. My friend has seen many more stings from them than I have."

"That's interesting. This woman lives in California. I wonder if her allergy was to this particular kind of bee. You're sure this is a bee sting and not the intentional injection of some substance that would cause this kind of reaction?"

"Oh, yes. The bee's stinger is still in the skin. We will also get a toxicology report, of course, just to make sure."

"Thanks, Doctor. We'll do our best to lighten your work load." Cara gave a head signal to Hank and they hurried out into the fresh air.

"*Apis mellifera,* the common honey bee," pronounced Professor Lightbody. He was holding a magnifying glass and looking at a tray on which was placed the bee the murderer had left on the table in Lou Saffron's room.

"Really? The Medical Examiner favored the killer bee," Cara said.

Lightbody was shaking his head. "This bee?"

"Well no not exactly. He thought the sting that caused the allergic reaction was that of a killer bee."

"Ah I see, that's quite different, isn't it? No question here: m*ellifera*."

Cara put her bee back in the plastic evidence envelope.

"We're thinking it would be unusual for one of these er. . . ah . . . *mellifera* to be flying around at this time of year."

"About that you'd be right."

Over lunch she told Byron the events of the morning and of her realization that Alonzo Schlink was standing out as a suspect.

"Where would he get a killer bee?" she pondered.

"Beats me." Byron answered. "Where would he get a honey bee, for that matter?"

"I'd like to search his house. Getting a search warrant on the indirect evidence I've got is unlikely."

"What would you expect to find?"

"Good question. I already know I'd find Halcion, so that's no help. Maybe he has a beehive in his basement. I'm kidding," she hurried to add. "But seriously, there could be books about bees, even some he recently purchased."

"You did a search of pharmacy records. Can't you do a search of bookstore records?"

"Fortunately, bookstores don't yet have to keep records of the books people buy—yet."

"Of course, and 'fortunately' is definitely the right word.

. . .

"He moves pretty fast for a fat guy, I'm talking about the guy in the ski mask who's snatching the garbage at night. Can't catch him to find out who he is. Bottom line—no stench and our members have missed a paycheck!"

The union rep was forced to give this discouraging report to the president of the local union.

"OK, let's compromise. Forget tenure . . . for now. We'll settle for the name change—Alternative Use Materials Specialists. When you talk to the men tell them that image is more important than job security. Get that into your conversations every chance you get."

. . .

It was usual for Byron to give Joan Arnold a list of books he wanted from the University Library, but Joan had a dental appointment and he needed to check the date of the first performance of *Coriolanus*. The date in his proofs seemed to him to be off by a year. So, he walked to the library building and entered the large reading room and headed toward the location in the stacks where he knew the reference book would be.

Sylvester Sleeves was walking toward him. They passed each other.

"Page."

"Sleeves."

Byron had an idea. He had suggested to Cara that she

search bookstore records for evidence that Schlink had bought books on bees. Maybe he'd taken them out of the library. He detoured to talk to one of the librarians.

"Good afternoon, Professor Page. What can I do for you?"

"Not for me, but for Alonzo Schlink. He asked me to check to see if the book on bees he'd requested was in."

The woman turned to her computer and began searching. After studying the screen she said, "No, please tell Professor Schlink we haven't been able to locate *Bees, Nature's First Social Climbers* yet."

That surprised Byron. The fact that Schlink had requested a book on bees was what he'd hoped to find, but "First Social Climbers" was not very murderous. Besides Schlink hadn't seen it yet.

"OK, thanks. I'll tell him." He started away from the desk.

"Oh," the librarian called after him, "You might tell Professor Schlink that the other books he took out are overdue."

Byron pivoted on his heel. "And, what books are they?"

She looked back at the screen. "*The Africanized Honey Bee: Death on the Wing, The Care of Bees in Laboratory Settings* and *Bee Sting, Symptoms and Emergency Treatment.*"

"Can you print that page?"

"Yes, of course."

"Please."

• • •

"Good work, Watson. You've done all the work for me." Cara said when she finished reading the sheet Byron had brought her from the library. "Of course it's circumstantial and by itself isn't enough to support an arrest, but it builds our case."

Byron was pleased he'd been able to supply something to lift her spirits, burdened as she was by three unsolved murders. The other thing he'd done was to take her out to dinner at Gratzi. The decibel level defeated normal conversation, but that and the room's continuous action made you know you were alive. The reason for all the people and the noise: the food was great. Certainly their conversation would be private. Even though they had to yell at each other, it was certain no one else could hear them.

"I don't want you to feel I'm taking over your case, Holmes," Byron reassured her. "There's plenty for you to do. Where did he get the bees? Find out if he bought some bees and you'll have more than circumstance."

"Yes, even if he bought a single bee, I'd have him. No jury would believe an English professor would do that in Ann Arbor in the winter for any purpose other than murder."

. . .

"A good administrator has a thousand eyes." Evita Lopez was pacing back and forth in the living room of the University President's House. "She . . . er . . . he must identify potential loci of problems before they develop." She paced, hands clasped behind her back, head pushed forward, just as she'd seen Napoleon doing in a movie. "He must never let his enemies steal a march on him."

"Steal a march?" Felix repeated baffled.

"ENEMIES. Who are your ENEMIES?" she demanded, looking down on Felix, legs spread—another pose from the movie.

Felix's mind became blank as it always did when she stood over him.

"Could you give me a hint? Sounds like?"

"OHH!" She tossed her head in exasperation. "THE REGENTS. THE REGENTS. They are your enemies. You must see that they have their spies everywhere, recording your every move, and NON-MOVE."

Felix glanced toward the window.

"You don't know do you? You don't know what's going on at the ice arena. Answer me!"

Felix's face twitched twice. "Skating?"

"Ho ho, so you know the ice arena is used for skating. There is a glimmer of hope. Yes, that is what will go on until the end of the first period of the Big Ten Championship game tonight. At that time the ice is re-surfaced by the Zamboni machine. Only tonight that won't happen, because our Zamboni is broken and the company can't fly one of their men here to repair it because the men refuse to stand in line for airport security checks. And, if you think you can solve this problem by flying a repairman here on one of our fanatical alumni's private jets, forget it, because our Zamboni driver, thinking he wouldn't be working tonight, took off to get in some ice fishing before the spring thaw. Now what do you say about that?"

"What's broken?"

"THE MACHINE! CAN'T YOU HEAR?"

"I meant . . . Yes dear."

.   .   .

The maize and blue and the green and white clad warriors skated off the ice. The score was tied 1 to 1. The tension was high. What would the second period hold for the shouting fans on each side? First the ice must be resurfaced.

The gate at the end of the arena opened and the Zamboni machine lurched onto the ice. It was making unusual noises and belching black, sooty smoke. A fat man wearing a stocking cap pulled down over his ears was driving. His bushy black moustache was somewhat askew. Spectators were wondering if they had ever seen a Zamboni driver wearing sunglasses before. The Zamboni was usually driven in a regular pattern of passes over the ice. This driver had a route of his own, corner-to-corner and round-and-round ending with a figure eight. One very unorthodox move was his head-on ramming of the rink walls. Lurching and belching the Zamboni left the ice.

A University of Michigan Regent sitting in the stands was appalled by the Zamboni's antics, but he forgot all about it when the Wolverines and Spartans skated back on the ice.

.   .   .

Byron called Cara as soon as he figured she'd gotten home from the restaurant. Lingering earlier over a shared *tiramisu* she'd described her experience of being called into her chief's office and told of the "help" he had arranged for her from the FBI and of the two agents' attempt to diss her. She'd said her boss, Kimbel, had been going along with the theory that the manner in which the authors were murdered was based on a salient feature of their literary work until she hadn't been able to explain what a bee sting had to do with Saffron's novels. Walking home from the restaurant, Byron had thought of a possible answer.

Cara answered the phone and immediately told Byron about the note she'd just read that was left for her by Jocie saying she was spending the night at her sister's to try to comfort her. There was still no word of Willie's whereabouts.

"It's a terrible thing. A person can't experience much greater terror than that of a parent with a missing child," Byron agreed.

"I tried to be upbeat with her today, but between us I'm very worried."

"You've got a lot on your plate. You're doing a great job—for everyone." Byron intended to be reassuring, but he was very concerned that the pressure had grown to a damaging level for the woman he loved.

"And I'm angry," Cara said. "On the way home I was thinking that those asshole feds are really a godsend, since they make a good target for my anger."

"Yes, I imagine they serve that purpose across the nation. I, however, called you because I had a thought that just might take away one of your problems."

"Be my guest."

"It began like this; I was walking home thinking what

a shame it would be if Lou Saffron's murder didn't follow the theme of her literary style. I guess it's the writer in me. I enjoy a creative plot. Anyway, something occurred to me, but I need some information."

"Like?"

"The chalked message on the table in Saffron's room; what were the positions of the arrow, the bee and the word 'SEE'?"

"Pardon me?"

"You said the bee was on the table and an arrow pointed to the bee plus there was the word. Was the arrow on the left side of the bee or the right and where was the word in relation to the bee?"

"Ah, I see what you mean," Cara said. "The arrow was on the left of the bee and pointing to it. Then came the bee and then the word. Why?"

Byron laughed. "I'm beginning to like this killer. He also likes a good plot. The *modus* of Saffron's murder *was* related to her novels. The arrow plus the bee means, 'A bee' plus 'See' equals 'A bee see!' A, B, C."

Cara visualized the table with the arrow the bee and the word. She made a loud kissing sound into the phone.

"I hope you heard that. It's great to be in love with a guy who likes a good plot."

• • •

Later that evening another tete-a-tete was taking place in the home of the University President. Maybe in its own way it was intended to be helpful as well. A very tired and bruised

Felix Lopez listened.

"I heard that the Zamboni driver showed up after all. The fish must not have been biting."

"Fish?"

Evita was used to Felix's failure to keep up with her. She changed the subject.

"So, what are you going to do about the war between Physical Anthropology, and Archeology?" Evita leveled this at Felix as if she were looking down a rifle barrel.

A very weary University President squinted at this interrogation. "War?"

"Can it be that you haven't heard about it? Everyone was talking about it at the Faculty Wives Club tea. The conflict has advanced to the point of physical pushing on the part of Physical Anthropology, and bloodshed is expected if Archeology retaliates . . . all those digging muscles."

"Is it over office space?" It was usually over office space, Felix thought.

"Office space? Of course not! It's over milk and salami!" Evita said this as if the dispute was as commonly familiar as the one over whale hunting.

Felix Lopez thought he had heard Evita say 'milk and salami' and since this made no sense he was sure his lack of sleep was causing random firings in his auditory cortex.

"Well?" Evita demanded.

Maybe he was asleep and having a bad dream, one of those in which you're never right no matter how hard you try.

"Your secretary called to say that they are coming to your office tomorrow for your judgment."

"They?"

"Physical Anthropology and Archeology! Can't you hear?"

Felix shook his head as if trying to get water out of his ear.

She continued, "It will take the wisdom of Solomon. Anthropology, of course, expects you to punish Archeology and Archeology knows you will side with them, the older discipline. Perhaps you'd like me to attend the meeting."

"No, no dearest, I know you have such a busy schedule, but perhaps you'd take a moment to review the problem in your own inimitable style. It would help me more than you can imagine."

Well that was better. Smiling now she began, "All right, it's like this. Anthro keeps milk for coffee and some lunchmeats for snacks in a refrigerator in an alcove off their conference room. They discovered the provisions were being stolen after they left for the day. One of them, who happened to be walking along the hallway to the Archeology Department, spotted a fragment of salami on the floor. An accusation was made. This was followed by an abusive rebuttal from the diggers. THEN, the next night, Archeology discovered that the goat's milk and hummus they keep in their own refrigerator was severely depleted. Shouting commenced, then name-calling and finally, as I said . . . pushing."

"How long has this been going on?"

"Almost a week. Each department has been replenishing its supplies and the next day discovers that the opposing faction has filched them during the night."

"No one has stayed after hours to catch the culprits?"

"They say it is beneath their dignity. They say that if

the burglary occurs just one more night, their gloves will be off. What I want to know is: What are you going to do?"

Felix, exhausted from nocturnal garbage collection, had begun to doze, but his long conditioning to Evita's demanding tone prompted a Pavlovian response of wakefulness.

"The salami . . . What kind do they buy?"

The fat man waited until 4 a.m. He was used to going out at that hour to collect garbage, but mercifully the strike had ended. He tiptoed up to the refrigerator in the Physical Anthropology Department. He looked inside. Yes, there was no doubt about it; only one slice of salami remained and only a drop of milk. Archeology had already performed their nightly filching. He reached into the bag he was carrying and took out several slices and placed them on top of the remaining slice in the refrigerator. He refilled the milk carton from one he'd brought. Onward to Archeology. Here, he saw that no more goat's milk remained and the hummus jar was empty. He made the replacements and tiptoed away.

13

The tractor-trailer trucks carrying all the electrical and control equipment for the ABC and NBC affiliate stations from Detroit were parked along the curb outside the League Building, their generators growling. The huge cables running along the ground from the trucks and through one of the side doors looked like hoses carrying air to competing deep-sea divers.

The media had arrived in rude force for this month's award dinner. The university had tried to block—at least limit—their entry, but it was like trying to keep termites out of a frame house on Orange Blossom Drive. While not being totally ignored, Dennis Duke's and I.B. Sames's lectures had not received major attention by the media, because at the time they occurred they had not yet been recognized as part of a serial killing. While this fact had become evident by the time of Lou Saffron's appearance, the media had been forced to pass up the lecture, because there were so many competing stories that week. First, there was Chelsea's elopement with a Bollywood dancer and then the astonishing revelation, through the discovery of secret, internal company documents, that Big Tobacco had instigated both World Wars. Motive? One investigator's opinion: "Profound fear or profound boredom means double-time puffing." Now, the nation's demand for brief news bites had turned to the approaching lecture by the blockbuster best-selling author, James

Parkinson. America was ready to give his anticipated murder its full attention. (The opening day of baseball was yet a week away and the NHL and NBA were merely putting in time until the play-offs.)

Parkinson, against the frantic advice of both his agent and publisher, was insisting on a show of cool indifference to the now much-publicized danger. What forced him to make his scheduled appearance in Ann Arbor was his own image of himself—that guide to most of our unfortunate decisions. Parkinson had come to think of himself as the swashbuckling hero of his own over-ripe novels. It would be unthinkable for his fictional hero, Rex Ross, to pass up public recognition of his accomplishments as a private eye because of wimpy threats. Besides, Parkinson was also counting on his own analysis of the *modus operandi* of the killer. It was his plan to 1) let nothing pass his lips except the bottled water he would carry in his pocket, and 2) avoid contact with sunflowers, his only and secret allergy. Plus, since the season for snowmen had passed, what real danger could there be?

Inside the auditorium, the English faculty once more assembled. On this occasion no one was late. While grumbling about the intrusion of crass commercialism into their *sanctum sanctorum,* they also felt a heightened excitement.

"James Parkinson; isn't he the guy who is only capable of producing those very short paragraphs?" asked Jack Sumner.

"Yes, do you think that applies to other aspects of his functioning?" wondered Ruth Hackett.

"If it does, just think of Proust's endurance," put in Andy Backus.

Nicole Truffaut, who taught Cinema Literature, critically viewed the lighting. It was much too strong. A backdrop, erected by the television crew in order to cover the distracting lines of the room's carved oak paneling, was much too white. Henry Beasley and the author would appear to be insect specimens wriggling on a porcelain laboratory dish.

Henry Beasley and James Parkinson climbed the steps to the podium and took seats behind a table arranged by the television directors. On the white backdrop the TV crew had just affixed a flag bearing the university's name and seal. The televised picture would now come across as a press conference at which the University of Michigan Athletic Director (Henry) would name a new football coach (Parkinson).

Faced with the imperious TV crew, Parkinson, in keeping with his internal image of himself as Rex Ross, looked bored and slightly amused. Beasley looked like a child who'd had his sucker snatched away and was helpless to re-grasp it. The TV director gave a countdown and pointed to Henry.

For a moment, Henry couldn't settle on an identity— English Department Chairman, Athletic Director or a suspect in a police line-up. What resulted was a combination of choice one and three, a guilty English professor. Thus he haltingly made the introduction of his famous guest, not boastfully as he would have liked, but apologetically as if he were unworthy of the honor.

That was OK with James Parkinson. His attitude said he had enjoyed much groveling in his presence. His attitude also said, "Let's cut to the chase." He was already smiling into the cameras and pulling the microphone away from Beasley before Henry could complete his remarks.

"Thanks, Doctor Measley, I'm happy to be back in Ann Arbor, back after many, I'm happy to say, successful years. My bus passed through here long ago on my way to Chicago. Ann Arbor was a half-hour stop. I got off the bus and talked this babe I'd been sitting next to into taking a walk. It was a rainy, blustery night. The blood-red lights of the State Theater marquee reflecting in the puddles on Liberty Street reminded me of Nam." He passed a surveying glance over the audience that said, "Of course, none of you draft dodgers would know anything about THAT."

He turned and looked at Henry as a principal might regard the winner of the eighth grade citizenship award.

"Doctor Measley, here, has provided me with classier transport this time and to show my appreciation I'm going to do something I've never done before. I'm going to read the opening chapter of my new book. It comes out in June and will be the selection of the Book of the Month Club, The Literary Guild and the Detective Book Club. $26.99 with that damned 30% discount."

Having announced this special treat, Parkinson now smiled at Henry like the busy father who expects his son to be grateful for his having showed up for the last quarter of the kid's soccer match. He turned, then, to stare soberly into the cameras for a long moment. It was a pause that was bulging with meaning—I'm in command here—I hope you can understand and appreciate the depth of what you're about to hear—Are you paying complete attention, because this will be a once-in-a-lifetime experience.

"*Blood Sausage,* Chapter One." This he pronounced in the same tone as a minister might read, "In the beginning."

We both had our guns out, held loosely across our laps. Wolfgang Flak's eyes, pale blue as Arctic ice, stared into mine. His expression was one of mild regret. For decades we two had crossed swords. Blood had been drawn on occasion, but we had resisted any final settlement; our rivalry had been too valuable to each of us. 'A man is as great as his greatest enemy,' someone once said. But we both knew this contest, like all good things, must end, and end it would any moment now.

Wolfgang was holding his Sig-Sauer ProSig. It was a famous piece, hand-built by Dieter Sauer himself and modified by the Reichsmeister Helmut Tod. The barrel rifling was secret and unmatchable—try as many gunsmiths had. The mold for the grip was taken from Flak's hand at the moment of orgasm—the moment of ultimate triumph and self-realization. Flak was confident and well he should be. His hand-eye co-ordination was legendary. His name was first on the scoreboard of every video game he had ever played. Soon he would make his move and it would be near the speed of light.

In my lap was my old Colt Python with the borings Wells Weatherby had drilled for me to lighten the beast. Consequently, thinned out as it was it could only be fired twice in succession without heat-warping the barrel. So far I'd managed with only one shot at each outing. My ammo was special. A fellow Nam grunt, an Oglala Sioux named Billy TwoFeathers, custom-made my cartridges. He'd married a Hopi woman and lives with her on Middle Mesa, she carving kachinas for the tourist trade and he crafting cartridges for a few—very few—appreciative and generous customers like me. My cartridges are Winchester 125gr. WinClear jacketed soft points to which Billy adds 20 extra grains of Supreme. But it is the other thing that Billy does that makes all the difference. He engraves into each bullet an individual Sioux greeting to the afterlife for the projectile's recipient. I liked to think this makes their crossing over smoother, easier.

I'd never measured my reaction time. A Vietcong woman who'd disarmed me, raped me and spared me, advised me it wasn't world class and I should pay a visit to Hung Dao, a Buddhist priest, who lived in a mountain top village in Myanmar. As soon as I could, I took that advice. I owe my life many times over to that woman's advice . . . and lust.

Hung Dao wouldn't accept me as an acolyte until he had observed me living in his village for a whole year. It was a year of hard labor in the fields working haunch by haunch with the natives. It was a year of emotional growth. At the end of it I was admitted into Dao's presence and became his student. He led me away from a focus on the material world, and showed me how to look beyond the world of illusion, the world Western man believed in, and into the actual world of 'mind.' He taught me that those who concentrate on matter sacrifice precious reaction time, because they place an unnecessary and delaying step in the path of their synaptic response.

I shifted my gaze, now, from Flak's eyes to a

point in the center of his forehead. I looked through his head and into my future. It was a future in which I didn't see Wolfgang Flak.

I was vaguely aware that Flak had moved. Aware, also, of the old Python rustling in my hand followed by a sound like distant thunder in an imagined land. But my concentration was on the large hole in Flak's forehead through which I saw the wall behind him where his brains were splashed like a plate of spaghetti marinara.

Parkinson looked up and out on a sea of gaping mouths.

"That's the first chapter of *Blood Sausage,* my twelfth novel. As I said, it will be in bookstores in time to take to the beach." He said this with an air of levity and expected laughter in response. Instead, the audience continued to stare as if they had just seen Henry Beasley flash them.

Beasley, belatedly realizing that Parkinson had finished speaking, grabbed the microphone and began the requisite, appreciative, and excessive claims of the honor paid the university and ending with the presentation of the plaque. Applause began like scattered raindrops on a tin roof, and then swelled briefly to rapidly diminish again to a few scattered drops.

Since he had decided not to eat or drink, his appearance at the dinner was to give his fans a chance to advance and pay homage. The faculty members, while grumbling among themselves, were by and large decent, empathic folk who felt an obligation to Beasley, so they came forward and paid homage . . . to the best of their abilities.

On his way out of the dining room and toward the Bell Tower Hotel a television reporter intercepted Parkinson and asked how he felt about going to sleep where two other authors had been murdered. He acted as if he had never thought of the issue.

"I've never had trouble sleeping," he replied thoughtfully, "Not even in Nam."

Also awaiting him were four members of the Ann Arbor Police SWAT team. They were assigned to escort him the three blocks to the hotel. This escort he vehemently refused.

"Hell, I haven't had a required escort since I was two and my mother made my older brother hold my hand crossing the street."

He wouldn't budge until the boys in blue packed up and left. Parkinson also declined to have Henry's company. He made the walk alone . . . except for the fat man who moved protectively from shadow to shadow along his route.

14

Cara had heard of Parkinson's macho refusal of protection before he came thorough the door of the hotel. To avoid an unneeded scene with him in the lobby, she had emptied it temporarily of the three detectives and four officers she'd requisitioned. She alone greeted Parkinson.

Looking around, seeing but her, he said, his face blanching and with obvious alarm, "Only you, Sergeant?"

"I waited until you returned to tell you about our arrangements for your transportation to the airport tomorrow morning. We've made a reservation for you with one of the cab companies. The university will pay, of course."

"No police escort?" An uncontrollable tremor produced a vibrato.

"We knew you were a man who hated people making a fuss. Since your plane departs at nine, I scheduled the taxi for seven to allow for airport security. You'll get a wake-up call at six?"

"Yeah, well . . . yeah."

"Good night then."

"You're going to stay here, aren't you?"

"I hadn't planned on it."

"Ah . . . well . . . good night," he said like a man left marooned on a desert island.

Parkinson headed toward the stairs.

"Oh, I think you'd better use the elevator, they're working on stairs—new treads," Cara hurried to say, preventing him from joining the seven officers crowded together there.

The moment the elevator ascended, the lobby once again became a scene of action. Tonight the university was paying for all the rooms on Parkinson's floor. It would be empty except for him. Again men were posted in the stairwells, in the alley and on the roof. An emergency medical room had been installed in the office behind the registration desk for pulmonary and cardiovascular life-support.

"You certainly went all out," commented Byron when Cara slipped down the half block to his house for a quick cup of coffee.

"The problem is, I thought I had the hotel covered the other times."

"Yeah, but the other two were women who didn't have the heft of James Parkinson. He may have a bloated idea of himself, but he looked to be pretty solid in the muscle department."

She relaxed. "I know you're right."

"Stay here tonight," Byron said. "It's way more comfortable than sitting in that lobby and if they need you, you can be there in twenty seconds flat."

"I'll stay a while, but I can't go to bed. I've got to check in now and then, if for no other reason than for the sake of morale."

"The general showing himself along the trenches?"

"Herself."

"Didn't I say that? OK, then, the general's aide-de-camp must make an appearance as well—two paces behind and one pace to the side."

Cara looked around. "Let's see, that places you on the radiator over there. I hope for your sake the heat has been turned down."

They talked for a while. Cara did rounds at the hotel and returned. They talked. Byron made coffee and cinnamon toast. Cara made rounds. They talked.

•   •   •

For several days now Felix Lopez had made his pre-dawn rounds of the refrigerators in the Physical Anthropology and Archeology Departments. Still the feud boiled. While each side conceded that in the morning the quantity of food was as it had been the night before, Anthropology claimed Archeology was stealing their higher priced, fine *filsette* and replacing it with coarse *calabrese* salami. The return claim was that the *tahini* in the *hummus* Anthropology was trying to pass off was rancid. In desperation, the fat man had bought a Middle-Eastern cookbook and was preparing to make his own *hummus*.

But in spite of their complaints, each side seemed to eat its fill. Every night Felix found both refrigerators badly depleted. If only he could get the food exactly right, he believed they would eventually abandon this silly tit-for-tat.

One night, his flashlight caught the glint of a reflection off a drop of liquid on the corridor floor in the Archeology building. He bent down and examined it closely; it was milk, but it was not along the course one would normally expect the feuding parties to take on their nightly raids. He followed the trail to the basement and along the tunnel leading to the Kelsey Museum of Archeology.

Here he paused. He saw a faint light along the crack at the bottom of a door on which was printed the word, Ossuarium, the bone room. Not sure what or whom he might encounter, he reached into his pocket for his false moustache and stuck it on. He quietly turned the doorknob and peeked in. Seated in a corner, reading a thick book by the light of a gooseneck lamp was a very pretty, young, blond girl who he made out to be about thirteen or fourteen. Beside her on the floor was a glass of milk. She read and munched on a sandwich.

Sensing someone else was in the room she looked up. She saw a very fat, mustachioed, balding man dressed in nondescript work clothes.

"Oh, it's you," she said. "I expected you'd make your way down here sometime."

"Really?"

"Look it's none of my business, but *really* this place should have been dusted ages ago. Luckily, one of the secretaries in Anthro has a huge bottle of Allegra in her desk."

The fat man closed the door behind him and came into the room. Immediately, he recognized that this was the missing teenager everyone was looking for.

"Whatcha reading?" he asked.

"*The Oxford Companion to Archeology*. It's super. Ever read it?"

"I don't think so. Looks like a lot of pages."

She flipped to the back. "Eight hundred forty-four, but

it reads like a Grisham."

"Hey, I like Grisham."

"Well, maybe not *just* like a Grisham. Don't rush out and buy it . . . maybe check it out of the library first."

"Thanks. You staying down here?"

She looked at him. Could she trust this janitor? He looked like an OK kind of guy.

"Yeah. For a whila."

"Cozy."

She smiled. He understood. "Yeah, right. Cozy."

"I know this none of *my* business, but I'm wondering if you've run away from home."

She did a motion with the shoulders that said, "Yeah, what can a girl do?"

"I ran away from home when I was about your age," the fat man said. "Hid out in the farmers' market." He laughed at the memory.

"Hey, that's cool. I get it, all the food you could eat. Cool."

"Yeah, but mostly what I could scrounge was vegetables and I was the opposite of a vegetarian, what ever that is."

"Carnivore."

"Excuse me?"

"You are, or at least were, a carnivore—meat eater."

"Son-of-a-gun! And I didn't even know it."

She laughed. "What's your name?"

"You can call me by my nickname, Pres."

"Mine's Willie. What's it like being a janitor?"

He thought about it. "Basically all jobs are alike. Depends on what you put into them."

"What's that mean?"

"Like take these professors. Some of them love their work and some of them feel they're stuck in the wrong job. I've been watching—know what I mean?"

Willie listened.

"I watch and what do I conclude? The ones who are putting themselves into the work are the ones who love it. The ones who are disgruntled are the ones who don't, ah . . . "

"Invest themselves?"

"Right outa my mouth. Me, I like doing a good job here. I think it's important when people—you know, kids coming to the museum to look at the Egyptian stuff—important they aren't looking through dirty glass on the display case. It makes a difference in how they feel about their visit . . . and . . . and about ancient Egypt."

Willie considered this. "How come you let this place get so dusty, then?"

"You're a sharp kid, you know that? You see right away what my weakness is . . . I'm scared of skeletons."

Willie was leaning on a box of skulls. She reached over and patted one. "I know there's no use telling you there's nothing to be afraid of. If you're afraid, you're afraid. My mother is always telling me how I *shouldn't* be feeling."

"You too? Mine did the same."

"You know, I think to myself, OK, I could have a kid someday and that will mean I'll become a mother. What I want to know is what the fuck happens, does a woman's brain melt when she's in labor?"

"Can't be that." the fat man said, "Father's brains melt too."

"Hey right, but not as bad as mothers."

"No? Ask a son."

"People say, 'Yeah, but your parents mean well.' It's just that they do such a piss-poor job of meaning well."

"You know I hadn't thought of it that way," the fat man said. "You're a deep thinker, you know that?"

"C'mon."

"I'll bet you could help the police solve these killings of famous writers. Have you had any ideas about that?"

"That's a slam dunk: jealousy."

"Jealousy. You think so?"

"When I was cut from the soccer team, it was all I could do to keep from tripping the team members on the stairs. Some writer who isn't famous feels the way I did, but he's not holding back."

"Wow, that's sharp thinking. I hope you write books someday and let people in on the way you think."

Willie thought about this and smiled.

"To change the subject a little," the fat man said, "Your mother doesn't know where you are. Right?"

Willie nodded.

"There's this other odd thing about mothers; they get real bent outa shape if one of their kids disappears. I guess they can't help it any more than I can help being afraid of skeletons."

"I know you're right Pres, but I'm not ready to go home. I'm only on page 624 and there are some parts I want to re-read." She held up the thick tome.

"Did you hear anybody here say anything about going home? Maybe if she just knew you were all right. Know what

I mean?"

The intimate emotional contact between them broke with Willie smiling in acquiescence and the fat man saying, "Gotta get back to work. I'll let this room go while you're still using it—stir up too much dust."

He went to the door and looked back.

"Stop by again," Willie said. "And, Pres, you won't tell anyone I'm here will you?"

The fat man smiled. "Honey, that's the *last* thing in this world I'll ever do."

•　•　•

Byron had passed through sleepiness into what felt like permanent wakefulness. It was light outside. Cara emerged from the bathroom after washing and reapplying her makeup. She looked wide-awake and fresh. Byron knew, however, that hers had been a tense vigil. She felt a heavy responsibility for the well-being of the haughty author who would be getting his wake-up call just about now.

"There is no taxi, by the way," Cara said picking up her purse. "I was always going to drive him to the airport."

She had a thought. "Why not come along? You could be the representative from the English Department. That would supply the note of homage he'd enjoy."

Byron weighed this proposal quickly. "Why not. I don't have classes today, and I'll have you all to myself on the way back."

Things were astir when the two entered the Bell Tower Hotel. Cara quickly walked up to the registration desk where a detective was giving orders to the clerk.

The clerk seeing Cara's approach began explaining to her, "I gave his room the 6:00 a.m. wake up call, but he didn't answer."

"I told him to try calling the room again," put in the detective.

Cara nodded to the deskman, who dialed again, listened and began shaking his head.

Cara's shoulder's sagged. "Let's go up and take a look."

Byron tagged along; all the others were too focused on their fears to notice. Cara opened Parkinson's door with a passkey. She and two of the other men entered the room. Byron slipped in and looked over their shoulders.

James Parkinson was sitting bolt upright in a chair about three feet from a wall. There appeared to be a large red hole in the center of his forehead. On the wall behind him was a huge splash of blood and what must have been his brains. The four of them viewed the gore, frozen in shock. Finally, Cara stepped forward to the body. Byron drew in a breath when he saw her touch the gaping hole with her finger . . . and smell it. She went behind Parkinson to the wall, where she touched the blood with her finger and *tasted* it.

"What a waste of a good spaghetti dinner," she said and then returning to look more closely at Parkinson's forehead. "This lipstick was borrowed from a blond with Spring coloring."

"You're kidding," let out one of the detectives.

"Actually, no . . . but he *is* dead. That's no joke." She stood thinking a moment and then added, "Joe, go down to the desk and call in the crime scene team. I don't want to touch this phone or anything else until they've been here."

"Right." He left.

Once more, Cara and the other detective began carefully searching the room. Byron, who had been standing still, was forgotten. Quietly he moved forward to get a closer look. The lipstick mark was about an inch in diameter. How easily our imagination will construct what we expect to see. He stepped past Parkinson's corpse to look at the mess on the wall. A plate of spaghetti—just like the first chapter of Parkinson's new book. Then an orange fleck in the sauce caught his eye. He leaned closer. He'd seen this sauce before. Where was it? He froze! He almost called out to Cara . . . but stopped. Had she noticed? Had she noticed and avoided saying anything in the presence of the other detectives?

Byron moved back near the door and waited until she, while passing him on her examination of the room, looked directly in his eyes. If she had recognized the sauce as he had, she'd certainly give him a knowing look.

She passed near him and said ruefully, "This guy is good. I feel like a sucker in a shell game." She continued with her survey of the room.

So, she hadn't remembered that she had seen the spaghetti sauce before—seen it, eaten it, and commented on its flavor—at his house. It was Pam Backus's sauce. Byron was sure. He had eaten it many times.

He walked over to Cara. "I'll be at my place. When you can, come over and I'll make us some breakfast."

"As soon as the photographers and the lab people get here I'll come over."

Leaving the hotel, Byron wasn't aware that the morning was unseasonably warm. He didn't notice the robin hopping about on the small area of grass in front of his porch. In fact, he walked past his front walk and almost to the corner before he caught himself. Was it true? Was that really Pam Backus's sauce? If so . . . No, it just couldn't be. Inside the house, he sank into the easy chair near his kitchen and tried to think it through.

The murderer had to have been at the lecture. There was no other way he could have known about Parkinson's chapter. Andy qualified. He sat next to Byron, and Byron remembered Andy had left early, skipping the dinner—said he had to help his son with a school science project. But how would Andy have been able to get into Parkinson's room at the Bell Tower Hotel? Wait a minute. Wasn't he jumping to a ridiculous conclusion just because he saw some carrots in spaghetti sauce? There must even be commercial brands with the same ingredients as Pam's. There must be, but he'd never seen any. And, what about motive? What motive would Andy have?

At that moment he experienced what qualified as an epiphany. He heard Andy's voice in his memory. It was in this very room the morning after Dennis Duke was murdered. Andy was claiming that since he had no ambition to write fiction he lacked the envy harbored by the other members of the faculty toward the best-selling authors. But now Byron knew that Andy had strong reason to be envious—he'd read the ten rejection letters Andy's mystery novel had received.

Byron shook his head. What was he thinking? This killer had to be mentally unbalanced and Andy was rock solid

. . . or was he? Ten rejection letters might tip even the soundest person over the edge.

Byron quickly went to the refrigerator. He still had part of a jar of Pam's marinara sauce. He took it out and spread it on a plate. He studied the shade of red, the aroma of the basil, onions and the garlic. Most telling, however, were the carrots. A distinctive ingredient in Pam's sauce was the addition of carrots cut into tiny triangles. Finally he tasted the sauce. He returned to the Bell Tower Hotel.

The lobby was busy with the various crime detection disciplines going about their work. Cara was sitting with three men around a table looking over a floor plan of the hotel. She didn't notice him. He ran up the stairs, behaving like one of the other busy professionals. He entered Parkinson's room. Three men from the Medical Examiner's office were trying to get Parkinson, who was frozen by rigor in the seated position, onto a stretcher for removal.

Byron was only interested in the red blotch on the wall. The crime lab people were busy dusting for fingerprints. They hadn't gotten around to the wall yet. Byron sidled over as if mildly curious, but all his powers of concentration and observation were at their peak. He assessed the color, the aroma, identified the tiny carrot triangles; finally he moistened his finger tip with saliva, checked to see that no one was looking and touched the red smear and put it in his mouth.

There was no doubt! It was the faint hint of anchovies that convinced him. It was Pam's sauce.

Byron quietly left the hotel and began walking and thinking. What should he do? He walked along the Diag past the place where the snowman had stood. Could easy-going

Andy, Andy who was always ready with a bright, humorous quip, have crouched here, lying in wait for the unsuspecting king of horror? The idea of it was staggering. It turned Byron's world upside down.

Standing there, he faced up to the fact that he must now decide what this newly formed suspicion demanded he do next. In all fairness to his friend, he should not reveal the source of the spaghetti sauce to anyone, not even to Cara, until he was absolutely sure of Andy's guilt. What could he do to be sure? He wandered back to his house, pondering the question.

Cara came and they had a quick breakfast. Byron had trouble keeping up his end of the conversation, so caught up was he in his own thoughts about Andy. Cara said the Medical Examiner was at that moment doing an expedited autopsy to determine the cause of Parkinson's death and she needed to go to the morgue to get the results as soon as possible. She kissed Byron and left, leaving him now able to devote his full attention to his huge dilemma.

An hour later Cara called him to say that the autopsy showed that Parkinson's death was caused by a myocardial infarct, an ordinary heart attack. It had not been murder after all.

Still, Byron knew that the scene had been set using Pam Backus's sauce. Logic dictated that it had to play a part in Parkinson's death. He needed to think. He did that best while walking.

15

Byron emerged from his total, inward focus on the problem of how to prove or disprove the ludicrous possibility that Andy was a serial killer to find that he had walked aimlessly to the grassy center of the Law Quadrangle. He saw a bench against one of the four walls and went to it. The warm, yellow stone of the neo-gothic structure surrounding him seemed to restrain him, telling him that he must decide on a course of action before he left this place. He must review each murder and pull out of that analysis the hard bit of evidence that would point to Andy . . . or by its absence prove his innocence.

Dennis Duke. How could Andy have convinced Duke, afraid of being alone at night as he was, to leave the safety of the Bell Tower Hotel? He had the opportunity to talk to Duke at the dinner, especially during the time afterward when people were coming up to speak to the author. Byron strained to remember the scene. Yes, perhaps he did see Andy by Duke's elbow. But, then he was gone. He was not there when Byron looked around for him as he left the dining room. Might Andy, leaving early, have seen the students pushing the top part of the snowman onto the slippery plastic? Did he recognize the unique opportunity this provided him? Dennis Duke carried a cell phone. Had Andy by some ruse obtained the number? Could he then have called and made a date to meet Duke in front of the snowman. Or better still, having established himself as a legitimate member of the faculty, Andy may have, during dinner, arranged for a meeting in some more conventional setting like Duke's room at the hotel, and then, recognizing the opportunity presented by the snowman, he could have called and told Duke of the students' wonderful creation, assuring him it was only a three-minute walk from the hotel. All this was possible, but if presented with an investment opportunity as iffy as this, Byron would venture no more than a nickel.

I.B. Sames. Killed by an overdose of Halcion. Finding a bottle of the drug in Andy's possession would constitute hard evidence. This wasn't likely. Certainly he would have thrown it away. That would be smart but, as the condition of his office bore witness, Andy seldom threw anything away. OK, where would the pills be? The office came naturally to mind. What else had been involved in that murder? Bondo. Andy could have put the Bondo in the door any time in the afternoon. Not too much of a problem there. So, finding a can of Bondo would be hard evidence. But how could Andy have gotten by the detectives that night?

Perhaps it was an essence in the air of the Law Quadrangle, air that for so many decades had flowed out of the classrooms surrounding it, air that had passed over the vocal chords of countless, brilliant, fledgling jurists making their irrefutable arguments, that led Byron to question a premise that was posing a difficult obstacle, the premise being that Andy had been outside the hotel faced with the problem of getting by the detectives and up to Sames's floor. Perhaps it wasn't necessary to get by them at all. Perhaps he was already there—already in one of the other rooms on Sames's floor.

Byron then recalled that he hadn't seen Andy at the dinner. He could have been in the kitchen putting the drug into her food. He'd have a problem doing that and not getting the attention of the catering staff. But suppose he managed that somehow. He could go straight to the hotel and go up to his own room before the police took up their posts to guard her. He could then wait until he felt sure the drug had produced its effect, tip-toe across the hall to enter her "unlocked" room, arrange the scene so she appeared to have died reading one of her books and then return to his own room. In the morning, at the moment he heard Cara and the others going into her room, he could have left, unnoticed in the hubbub that followed.

Bondo. As Byron remembered from his jalopy repairing days, you had to use everything in the can, because once the curing agent was added, the whole batch set up like a rock in a matter of minutes. Why keep a can of rock-hard Bondo? Still, where would it be if Andy had kept it? His office.

OK, so much for I.B. Sames. What about Lou Saffron? The bee was the only hard evidence—and the yellow chalk. Byron shook his head at the thought of Andy keeping bees in his office. But God only knew what was under that rubble. Andy would have the same problem of getting past the detectives in the lobby. This time, however, Cara had photographed all the other guests, so if Andy was already in one of the rooms when Saffron went up to bed, he'd have to be in one of the pictures.

James Parkinson. Cara had just told him that the autopsy revealed a myocardial infarct as the cause of death.

While it is a common, and a so-called "natural" way to die, something usually causes it, brings it on: physical exertion, wild sex, or emotional stress like disturbing news, or fear . . . That's it! FEAR! That was the answer. Parkinson must have been frightened to death. What would have frightened Parkinson so badly? Byron laughed out loud at the thing that came to mind—Wolfgang Flak. No, no, that wasn't right. Rex Ross wasn't afraid of Flak so Parkinson wouldn't be either. Then the truth came with a jolt such as a man might experience when he realizes he's accidentally walked into the women's restroom. Parkinson would be afraid of Rex Ross! Byron hit the side of his head with the base of his hand. This bizarre thinking was making him dizzy.

Byron took a deep breath and brought his attention back to the present. It was a glorious day. Young, healthy students walked busily along the sidewalk past his bench. No more dizzy flights of fancy; he must try to arrive at solid conclusions. One—he must search Andy's office. Two—he had to look at the photographs of the other hotel guests on the night of Lou Saffron's murder. He'd go back to the hotel now while there was still some degree of chaos and see if there was a chance to accomplish task number two. This evening, after Andy went home, he would take care of number one.

Striding with a purpose, Byron was back at the Bell Tower Hotel in five minutes. In the lobby were several small groups of police and other official-looking types in quiet conversations typical of an aftermath scene. The desk clerk, Byron noticed, was busy on the phone. Byron went straight to a stairway door and bounded up to the second floor. He waited there for a couple of minutes, giving the clerk time to finish his call, and then went to the elevators and punched the down button.

The elevator doors opened in the lobby and Byron was pleased to see the desk clerk glance over and see him emerge and walk directly toward him.

"We need to take a look at the pictures that were made of the guests last month when Lou Saffron died here. Sergeant Bartoli said you had copies of them in your office."

It was a shot in the dark, but not a problem if the clerk denied having the pictures. Byron was prepared to say, "Oh, she must have been mistaken," and leave. Instead, the clerk said, "Just a minute."

Byron followed the young man into the inner office behind the reception desk. He did not want to be seen going over the pictures where those in the lobby could see and remember him.

The clerk went to a filing cabinet where he took out a folder and turned, surprised to see Byron standing there.

"Thanks," Byron said, taking the folder and opening it on an office desk. "I'll call you when I'm through," he said dismissively.

Byron looked down at a sheet of paper listing the names and addresses of Lou Saffron's fellow hotel guests. A quick scan told him that, except for four rooms occupied by couples with no indication of an academic affiliation, the citizens of that international nation called Academia had booked the other twenty rooms of the small hotel. Andy Backus's was not among the names. But, then Andy wouldn't have used his own name.

Next came the photographs. On his first pass through the pile

Byron didn't recognize Andy and his heart lightened. Something made him go through the pictures again, more carefully. In spite of a masterful job done with a false beard, wig and puffed-out cheeks, this time Byron saw his old and dearest friend in the person of Professor Maurice DuPont of the Sorbonne. SHIT!

Byron pocketed the picture, closed the folder and unobtrusively left the hotel. Now what was he to do? The next thought was a relief. He didn't need to decide what to do until he had completed task number two, the search of Andy's office.

16

Byron had the key out and was aiming it toward Andy's door lock when another faculty member emerged from her office farther down the hall and headed his way. Quickly he adjusted his motion to a knock on Andy's door and did the facial equivalent of, "I guess he's gone for the day," and crossed the hall to his own room.

He waited a couple of minutes and scanned the hallway again. All clear. This time he gained his objective. He leaned on the inside of Andy's door and surveyed the landscape of papers, the mountains and valleys of files and books and boxes. Where to start? His previous deductive work told him he was looking for a bottle of Halcion, a Bondo can, something to do with bees, possibly a gun that would have scared Parkinson to death. What else? Oh yes, yellow chalk. It was like a scavenger hunt. He reminded himself he had always been good at that. His prowess, in fact, so impressed the woman he was paired with at a college party that he ended up collecting dividends not mentioned on the scavenger list.

He knew he must follow a plan. Peeking under a pile of papers here and rummaging through a box over there would yield uncertain results. He decided to begin where he stood and cover the room clockwise. Half an hour's effort produced nothing but frustration and sneezing. Two towers of papers had toppled and required careful restacking to avoid a recurring avalanche. He was considering abandoning the project when, needing a rest, he slid into Andy's desk chair. Looking at him, begging to have attention paid it like a friendly dog, was the screen saver of Andy's computer, a swirling porridge of the names of eighteenth-century English authors. Byron hit the space key and the authors vanished and he was looking at the Windows desktop. OK, where to start? He always started with his e-mail so he clicked onto the university web server, pointed to the Outlook Express logo and clicked.

As the listing of mail in the in-box appeared, Byron felt pangs of guilt. What right had he to invade his friend's privacy in such a flagrant manner? A reminder stepped forward almost as quickly; the fact that the spaghetti sauce was certainly Pam Backus's and there was no doubt that the bogus Professor Maurice DuPont was unquestionably Andy.

There were only a few items in the in-box, and all had been read but not erased. Byron double clicked one of them. It was from a company calling itself Science Resource.

"Dear Dr. Backus:

In answer to your request for an Egyptian asp, such as the Egyptian cobra, *Naja haje*, I regret to inform you that this reptile is in very short supply due to the pollution of its habitat, the Nile River. There are other North African asps, specifically, the puff adder, *Bitis arietans*, which might be obtained, but not in the time restraints you mentioned in your earlier communication. May we suggest an American native reptile such as *Micrurius fulvius fulvius*, the eastern coral snake? We are able to supply this specimen with five days notice. We hope we can assist you in your current research project.

Sincerely,

Herbert Rowbottom, Director

An asp? Why would . . . of course. The final author in Beasley's program was to be the author of a mystery series set in ancient Egypt, Elspeth Isis, a lady who had more books in print than the phone company. Andy was planning to kill her *a la* Cleopatra with the "sting of an asp."

There was nothing more of note in the column. Byron looked at the "deleted items" category: 643 messages still stored there. Andy's e-mail housekeeping was as bad as his office. Byron clicked on the category, and started reading backward in time.

February 14th, "UK Airgun Replicas. We are confirming your order for item # 333 Replica Colt Python 6" .357 Magnum. Shipping # 248876"

Byron had a thought and went to the "sent items" category. "February 10th, I wish to order your item #333, Colt Python 6" .357 Magnum. Please charge my Visa card # 330465978321 for the amount of 73 pounds."

Back to the "deleted items" file. A shipping notice from Biological Research Inc., confirming the shipment of three Africanized honey bees on March 5th. Following this was another shipment order from Apiculture.com for an observation hive of *Apis melliflerus*. Both were shipped to an address in near-by Chelsea, Michigan.

He scrolled back until he saw a shipping notice from Alibris for eight used books, one written by each of the scheduled authors, the four who had died and the three who'd cancelled and the one who remained to come, Elspeth Isis.

So Andy had bought books from a source that he thought wouldn't be as likely traced as the local bookstore sales records.

All of this e-mail correspondence added up to the fact that Andy had purchased a replica gun and some bees. Could they be here in the office? That's what I'm here for, Byron reminded himself. His purpose recharged, he resumed his search. At the end of the desk was a mound of books, five books long by four wide by ten high. What Byron was looking for couldn't be there. He started to pass by the pile when, trying to avoid toppling a stack of old exam papers, he lost his balance and put his hand down on the books to catch himself. The books in the center of the pile slid easily to one side revealing a cardboard box beneath them. The cube of books had a hollow core. Were the books arranged in this way to hide the box? It certainly looked like it. With dread, Byron lifted the cardboard flaps of the lid.

"Jesus!"

It was as if he were looking into the face of death: a huge, very real looking revolver—the Colt Python, an empty Bondo can, a partially empty medication bottle labeled "Halcion." Deeper in the box lay the disguise worn by Dr. Maurice DuPont, a bottle with air holes in the lid and a chef's jacket bearing the embroidered words, "University Catering.

"My God," thought Byron, "This must be how he was able to put the Halcion in I.B. Sames's dessert."

Below the jacket lay the mangy looking stocking cap worn by the "derelict of the Diag. From the very bottom of the box Byron lifted out a piece of bright yellow chalk and a strange looking set of pointed probes gathered on a key ring.

"Lock picks!" Byron murmured.

He now possessed the total truth. Andy Backus was the murderer of Dennis Duke, I.B Sames, Lou Saffron and James Parkinson. And, he was planning the dispatch of Elspeth Isis to the regions of the underworld. Just what he was planning in that regard wasn't certain, because there was no follow-up on the asp correspondence. Thank God for that, Bryan thought, or he might have been greeted with a pair of fangs when he'd put his hand into the box.

With a dry mouth, pounding heart and deeply saddened, Byron stood at the door of the office and looked back at the room. He would never view it again with amused indulgence as he had for so long. It was now a murderer's den. He was badly shaken. Good old fun-loving Andy. Andy, who was everybody's friend, was a cold blooded, premeditated murderer.

•   •   •

Wilhemina Droost was in the same corner as the night before. She had the thick book on her lap.

"Hi, Pres. I'm glad you came down, I've written a letter to my mother like you suggested."

"Good." The fat man sat down on a mummified crocodile.

"There's this problem."

"What's that?"

"See, I could go out and mail it, but I'm afraid that if it's mailed here in town the police will have someway to zero right in on the Museum. They've got all this electronic Star Wars shit."

"Yeah, you've got a point."

"I was hoping you would take it and drop it in a mailbox in the burbs."

"I've got a better idea," the fat man said. "I got this friend who's going to the Dearborn campus tomorrow. He could mail it from there."

"Cool. He wouldn't mind?"

"Not him." It was the fat man himself who had to be at the university's Dearborn campus the next day. He gestured toward the book. "What page you on, now?"

"709. You'd like it. It makes you feel like you're right there digging with them. It would be the coolest thing to discover your own hidden city—one that no one dreamed was there."

"Yeah, I understand, but me an' diggin'. You see I got this bad back. I think I better stay right here in the museum."

"Hey, what about this! Me out there finding all this great gold jewelry and statues and sending them back here and you taking care of it."

"I like that. We'd be a kind of archeological team."

She acted out an affected academic pose and speaking through her nose she said, "Ladies and gentlemen it is our distinct honor to have as our distinguished speakers this evening that renowned archeological team Willie and Pres."

The fat man doubled over laughing. "I can see it. I can see it." His attitude sobered, suddenly. "Don't you think Pres and Willie sounds better?"

· · ·

Byron left Angell Hall and walked in a daze onto the sidewalk along State Street. What was he going to do? How could he understand what Andy had done? He thought he knew his friend well, but the view of him he'd just formed was unnatural, phantasmagoric. Byron always did his best thinking when he took long walks. As a child his first consciously probing reflections had occurred walking behind the family's lawnmower. He'd composed his first poem cutting that expanse of grass, which had meant so much to his mother's sense of status. He walked now without destination into the cold night.

He walked and thought until becoming chilled, he stopped at a coffee shop on Main Street. His understanding had progressed thus far; Andy, by failing to be recognized as a writer of worth, had suffered a severe identity crisis. In his soul he was a writer, but these editors were telling him he was not. For an artist this was like having your mother deny your kinship. He had been able to bear the rejection until Beasley announced the lecture series, which would honor the very writers who were his enemies, those who had stolen the place that was rightfully his, the place at his mother's knee . . . so to speak.

As lunatic as his actions had been, the murders must have seemed to be the only direct, honest response open to him.

Byron dipped a biscotti in his coffee and took a bite before he reached the inevitable conclusion; the publishing business, by ignoring Andy's fine novel and pumping instead such drek into the marketplace, had created in Andy's mind the grounds for—JUSTIFIABLE HOMOCIDE. Andy experienced himself as an innocent victim of the "new world" of publishing. Byron felt empathic towards Andy's emotional state . . . still . . . Byron had to admit , . . killing was wrong.

Byron left the coffee house and began walking again. He still had to deal with the question of what he was going to do. On Hill Street he met a group of students so engrossed in their hilarity that they crowded him off the sidewalk and into a bed of daffodils, continuing then on their merry way completely unaware of the now-muddied Humphrey Professor of Shakespeare they had left in their wake.

Byron's feet were wet, but he hardly noticed. He was only vaguely aware of passing East Quad.

On the stretch of his walk from the corner of Hill and Washtenaw to the corner of East and South U, he had brought himself to definitively deal with the question of what he must do. He had had little direct experience with issues of crime and punishment. He had had a student a few years ago who had turned in a paper the greater part of which had been plagiarized. He had given the paper a failing grade, because she had chosen such poorly written stuff to steal. Of course, he had also required another paper of her very own. She ended up graduating with honors, and, according to a letter he had received at Christmas, she was now teaching English at Columbia.

Byron knew that social convention demanded that he turn Andy in for punishment. In this case that would mean incarceration for a very long time—maybe his natural life. But, Byron asked himself, what would Andy's incarceration realistically accomplish? First, the families of the victims could enjoy a momentary satisfaction of that primitive urge to get even. An eye for an eye. Secondly, Andy would be prevented from dispatching anymore best-selling mystery writers. Byron thought hard, but could not think of another benefit that would be realized by Andy's imprisonment.

Byron walked on and began considering the down side of punishment. First, and maybe most importantly, it would not bring back the dead. Secondly, it would ruin Andy's life and that of his wife, Pam, and also that of his kids. And what of Andy's students? Five times he had been voted the best teacher in the English Department. A lifetime behind bars would also cost the state a bundle. The scale was tipping in favor of no punishment.

So, if he didn't pass on what he had discovered to Cara, what then? If he disregarded the demand of the victims' families for revenge, a base impulse in Byron's view, he was still left with the imperative need to prevent Andy from killing anyone else. Byron was certain that his friend was not a danger to the general public. After all, he only killed best-selling mystery writers—and perhaps editors who had rejected his novel. Still, even this type of person must be protected. Could he think of a way to accomplish this short of imprisonment?

Byron stopped abruptly, standing in the center of the sidewalk, completely unaware of students who now had to detour around him. He had left one of the major purposes of punishment off his list—remorse. With punishment comes an admission of guilt and repentance . . . or does it?

Does one feel, *true* remorse, not just the feeling of guilt, but the recognition that one has violated the rights of others, leading to a changed concept of one's self? Or is the feeling produced by punishment just the shame of being rejected by others and the regret that one has fucked up and caused one's self all this trouble—self-pity in other words? Might true remorse be better achieved without the burden of shame and the pain of imprisonment? Perhaps punishment even played a part in recidivism? You did this to me, now I'll do this back to you. Tit for tat *ad infinitum.*

These were heavy questions and not ones Byron welcomed. He would much rather think of his forthcoming book and his marriage. But like a new parent, who had not really bargained for having to take on the total responsibility for the welfare of another human being, Byron soberly accepted the fact that this nevertheless was the case: his was the responsibility.. If he turned Andy in, Andy's life would be ruined. If he didn't and Andy killed Elspeth Isis it would be his, Byron's, fault.

He began to walk on. The problem he faced had become clear. In order to follow his reasoning and reject the conventional demand for punishment, he must come up with a foolproof plan to guarantee that all best-selling mystery writers would be safe—from Andy, at least. Others no doubt harbored the same urge to rid the world of them.

Byron passed through the Engineering Arch and onto the Diag. He walked slowly, cudgeling his brain to come up with a plan, and by the time he climbed the front steps of his house he had evolved what he believed to be a brilliant way to guarantee that Andy's life of crime was at an end.

He recalled one of his students having mentioned a midnight visit to a copy shop. He consulted his telephone directory and was pleased to see that the shop nearest his home stayed open late enough to meet his immediate need.

It was now ten o'clock as he stood before the door to the main entrance of Angell Hall. He entered the building and signed in with the guard. Nothing unusual about a professor returning to his office to get some papers that he discovered he wanted. He checked the other names on the list. Andy's was absent.

Byron went up to his office and emptied the briefcase he had brought with him. Empty briefcase in hand, he crossed the hall and knocked on Andy's door. No answer. Quickly now Byron went in and straight to the box containing the manuscript of Andy's mystery novel and put it in his briefcase. He then gathered up the completed proof of his own book that lay hidden beneath the paper-covered chair and added it to the briefcase. Checking repeatedly that he wasn't being followed, he hurried the four blocks to the copy shop. When a copy was made of Andy's book, he returned to Angell Hall where he returned Andy's original manuscript to its hiding place. He was back home again by 11:32. In his briefcase was a copy of Andy's *Breach of Confidence* and the final proof of *Please Let Me Introduce Mr. William Shakespeare*.

•　　•　　•

At 11 a.m. the next morning, a cab pulled to the curb in front of 318 S. Thayer Street. Byron was waiting. He'd not called a cab until moments before this. He didn't want to give the person or persons who had broken into his office an opportunity to plan some kind of a hijacking. It was only when inside the cab that he told the driver his destination, Detroit Metropolitan Airport. There he met Howard Forsythe, his editor, outside the security checkpoint and handed him a package containing Andy's and his manuscripts.

"Here they are. You're doing me a great favor and I appreciate it, but I sincerely believe you'll be thanking me once Andy Backus's book hits the bookstores."

"Don't mention it. By bringing me the Shakespeare book you've earned many favors from me."

Byron smiled. "Now don't forget our deal. You are also committing your house to publish any other novel that Backus may send you in the future."

Forsythe smiled in return. "I remember. I also remember what I'm to write in my letter accepting the book for publication that it was sent to me by a friend at Pindar Press, because they don't publish mysteries. The friend thought I'd be interested."

"That's it. One of the rejection letters Andy received was from them and so he'll believe it."

Byron looked around, scanning the crowd for someone suspicious. "You going to be safe with the proofs?"

Forsythe motioned with his head toward a very large man wearing a Yankees jacket on the other side of the security barrier. "A New York cop came along for an off-duty ride."

17

The Droost kitchen, spotless, every surface bright as a new penny, was flooded with mid-morning spring light. On the kitchen table were two cups of coffee. Tightly gripping the handles of each were two very similar right hands. Attached to the hands were the Jackson sisters, Jocelyn and Jane. An envelope was lying on the table between them, and they were staring at it as if it might levitate at any moment.

Earlier, Jane had picked up the envelope, delivered in the morning mail, and was starting to open it when Jocie shouted, "Stop! There's something fishy about this letter. There's no return address. It's printed on a computer printer. It has a hand-applied first class stamp."

This degree of wariness had been produced by days of expecting a ransom note from imagined abductors.

"If it were from a business, there'd be a return address. Ditto a letter from a friend, unless it is so casual a message they'd leave it off. In that case, wouldn't they address it by hand? Besides, we don't know anyone in Dearborn and the letter has a Dearborn postmark. And those tricky soliciting letters that are designed to look like a social letter—they don't lick a stamp and put it on crooked like this one."

"So, what should we do?"

"Call Cara."

Cara said she'd slide by the Droost house and take a

gander. True to her word, within fifteen minutes she came through the side door calling out, "Hello." Now there were three young women staring at an innocent looking envelope.

"Bring me a pair of scissors," Cara said picking it up. "There will be nothing useful on the outside. It's been handled by a number of people already."

Jane handed her the scissors.

"I'll cut the end off. What we want to preserve is the glued flap. If it was licked there may be useful information." She opened her purse and took out a plastic glove and withdrew the letter and spread it on the table.

"Don't worry none you daughter is unharm. She sends her love. Just so you no this is no a trick she says that Tuesday is her reglar night for piano lesson. She will be safe as long as you follow our destructions. NOT TRY TO FIND HER! We will take care of her like was one of our daughters. Ransom directions coming."

Jane started to shriek. Jocie grabbed her and hugged her. Cara soberly pondered the situation.

Willie, sitting at a computer upstairs in the Kelsey Museum two nights before, had carefully composed her letter home. She knew it wasn't the letter her new friend ,Pres, had in mind, but she thought it served her purpose better. She had wanted to tell her mother she was well, but she wanted to discourage any attempt to find her. She also wanted to establish that returning home immediately was not one of her options: she had been abducted! She didn't want her abductors' poor English to suggest a lack of intelligence—the police must not be tempted to think they could outwit the kidnappers—but rather to come to the conclusion that it was due to English being a poorly learned second language. For the proof of authenticity she came up with something only she would know. She didn't even think her piano teacher knew about her lesson since she dozed through the whole of it. The item she was most proud of was misspelling "instructions." "Destruction," was in keeping with the second language bit, but it was more. The smart police would realize the error showed the kidnappers' underlying potential for violence. They meant business! She had luckily thought to mention ransom at the last moment. What kidnapper would not include that?

Jocie calmed Jane by repeating the abductors' promise that there'd be no harm done.

"Oh, we must do as they say. We must not try to find her." Jane cried.

"Jane," Cara interrupted, "I'm afraid this is out of our hands now. This is a kidnapping and that's a federal crime. I have to report this to the FBI office in Detroit."

"Oh no, not the FBI," Jane moaned as if any hope for Willie had just been extinguished.

Cara had her own sour feelings about the FBI, specifically the two agents, who were this very minute working to embarrass her.

"Jane, be reasonable, they know what they're doing. Kidnapping cases are their specialty."

Jane continued to sob quietly and Jocie continued to hug her as Cara carefully re-inserted the letter in its envelope and left to contact the feds.

As Cara had predicted, the Bureau analyzed the letter with consummate skill and expedition. Within twenty-four hours they narrowed the suspects down to Iraqis living in Dearborn. The vital clue was the trace of *tahini* in the saliva of the person who had licked the envelope flap and the postmark. *Tahini* equals the Middle East? Dearborn is the largest Islamic community in America. Start with an evil deed, add the Middle East, what does that equal—the Iraqis or Iranians. The FBI, of course, had a list of all who lived in Dearborn. At this point the Department of Homeland Security preempted the case. In no time it amassed its forces for a grand midnight raid. Before they could act, however, an order to halt came from the Middle East desk at the State Department, where their expert read, "we will take care of her like was one of our daughters" to mean that Willie had symbolically been accepted into the bosom of a family. In the Islamic culture, the expert advised, this amounted to a sacred pledge of succor and protection.

In other words, Willie's welfare was assured as long as other parties observed the conditions of the pledge, "NOT TRY TO FIND HER." If, however, the conditions were ignored, all bets were off. Homeland Security found itself stymied.

The bottom line—Willie was going to be left alone—for a while, at least—to finish her book.

18

The nightly *tete-a-tete* in the bone room had become a regular, eagerly anticipated part of the day for both of them. Pres brought a thermos of coffee and tonight, donuts.

"My wife doesn't want me to eat donuts—saturated fat galore. She's totally right. But, still . . . once in a while."

"What's your wife like?" asked Willy, enjoying her donut.

"My wife is unique, a perfect example of her type. I am in awe of my wife."

Willie, surprised, studied Pres's face. She had never heard anyone speak of a spouse in those terms.

"You mean she's really beautiful?"

He nodded. "That, but much more."

Willie was very pleased with this. She saw a new dimension in her friend.

"What does your wife do?"

"Ah, what does my wife do? Many things, things that don't fit any category, but I guess most people would say she's a housewife."

Willie said in a pensive tone, "Me, I've decided I want to be an archeologist, but there are so many obstacles."

"Like what?"

"First of all, my parents. They would consider it frivolous. They both *know* I'm going to be a doctor. Now, *that's* important! B-O-R-ING."

"So, they'll get used to it."

"You don't know my parents. They would consider themselves negligent if they let me pursue something 'unimportant'. They'd withhold money, like totally"

"Maybe you just have to go it on your own," said the fat man.

"But, their obstruction is just one obstacle. There's language. From what I'm reading I can see it's important for an archeologist to be able to read Latin and Greek and other ancient languages. I have my doubts about my ability to do that."

"Obstacles, huh? Odd you should put it like that, cause that's kinda like what I see life to be, an obstacle course. You see when I was at training camp in the army we had to run these obstacle courses. They timed you to see how fast you could get through. You'd start running and there'd be this wall. You'd have to figure out how to get over—pull over a barrel, lean a plank against the wall. You'd run on and here was a pond—too deep to wade and keep your pack dry. So, wait for a buddy, get him on your shoulders, he'd have both packs and you'd wade across. Then a deep ditch . . . you get the picture, right?"

Willie was smiling at her friend's enthusiasm.

"Yeah, I understand—a challenge."

"What I'm trying to tell you is that most of the guys thought it was a pain in the ass. Why did the army have to give them a hard time? I thought it was a ball. I still do. That's what I think life is, one great, exciting obstacle course—one challenge after another. That's what's so great, life taking the time to give me, Pres, so many . . . well, listen to me. You'd think I was sellin' somethin'. Time to get back to work. I'll see you tomorrow, but no donuts . . . once in a while, know what I mean?"

"Oh, I almost forgot. I wrote another letter to my mother. Would you ask your friend to mail this one from Dearborn, too?"

"Sure, kid. Good night."

Willie, bemused by Pres's excitement, settled down on the thick pad of burlap sacks that was her bed.

The letter wasn't opened until it was at FBI headquarters in Detroit. Once again it bore a Dearborn postmark. Carefully it was placed on a sterile surface. Carefully it was unfolded.

This our ransom demand. Dr. Droost got to send check for $50,000 to United Nations Children's Fund. Fund must be on TV holding up bank paper proving deposit. Do this and child live. No do this and no live."

Immediately and efficiently the machinery of sophisticated analysis started up. Same paper, same printer, stamp from the same printing run. A slightly different composition of *tahini* was detected in the saliva on the envelope flap. The chemist forced to describe the difference could only come up with an unscientific, "less rancid." Next the linguistic expert affirmed that the note had the same author, but also noted that there was a decided deterioration in the English, especially evident in the last sentence. This must be due to the stress the kidnappers were feeling. The psychologist warned that this could be a sign of a dangerous mental decompensation. Once this occurs, kidnappers who had previously been able to think and act rationally—panicked. The demands must be met quickly.

The demand became the subject of a high level Justice Department special meeting. It was not what anyone had expected. A demand for a large amount of cash in unmarked bills would not have raised an eyebrow. The cash, in that case, would, of course, be destined for subversive Iraqi or Iranian plots. But the demand in the ransom letter was a puzzler. The meeting was concluded with the appointment of a committee and the Attorney General's directive, "Put the United Nations Children's Fund on the subversive list."

The agent in charge of orchestrating the payment of the ransom set up an emergency television broadcast in which Dr. Droost would be seen handing a representative of the Fund a check for $50,000. Luckily, one of his rivals at Homeland Security, ever watchful for an opportunity to find fault with a rival, caught the potentially fatal mistake—the ransom note had specified a deposit slip proving the Children's Fund now really HAD the money.

Willie had worked on the ransom note for a considerable time in the dim, pre-dawn light at the computer in the museum secretary's office. Across the street, the outline of Angell Hall was taking shape. She couldn't delay too much longer. She had been pondering what to put in the note, because, given this chance to demand anything she might want—a game we all play in our imagination from time to time—she was forced to face the limits of the possibilities.

The first thing that had come to mind was a statement like, "Release Willie from piano lessons." There could be no doubt about the note's author if she wrote that! The same went for, "Let Willie be an archeologist," or "Put money in escrow (she actually knew the term) for Willie to spend any way she pleases for her education." Here was this chance of a lifetime and she didn't dare to ask for anything for herself. Next, she considered, "Give $50,000 to the Kelsey Museum." She amended that to read, "Give $40,000 to the Kelsey and $10,000 to the janitor named Pres." These demands, also, would likely give the game away. It had to be something more remote; she'd heard the term, "arm's length." Something remote from herself, and yet something she cared about. She had arrived at fifty grand as a sum high enough to be a credible ransom demand while being something she thought her father could afford. He would have quickly set her straight on this if he'd realized he was making a donation rather than paying a ransom to save her life.

Tension mounted unbearably as the Droosts, their friends and all of the feds waited for the kidnapper's second demand. The only question was, which subversive UN fund would be the recipient—the project to outlaw landmines was a favorite guess or perhaps the initiative to ban capital punishment for minors.

On the next day's eleven o'clock news, a smiling UN worker waved the deposit slip and held it for a camera close-up. At mid-morning the next day, the screen door of the Droost's kitchen slammed and a familiar voice yelled out, "Anybody home, I haven't had any breakfast."

So swift was the response of the de-briefing team that this acutely felt request for food was ignored and Willie was whisked off to the University of Michigan Hospital for a complete examination. On the evening news, viewers across the nation watched and heard the Chairman of Internal Medicine—wearing a white lab coat, which he otherwise never wore—describe the medical team's findings.

"Of course what I will tell you is subject to modification pending further studies and consequently does not constitute the definitive, final, nor single possible, conclusion. But, based on the clinical evidence obtainable at this time, but possibly modified at a later date, we found that Wilhemina Droost has . . . er . . . ah . . . gained weight."

The informational de-briefing was exhaustive. The especially selected female psychologist grilled Willie for hours. Anticipation was written on the faces of the waiting agents who encircled the psychologist when she finally emerged from the interrogation room. She answered their expectant faces with a summary, "Shit!"

Willie wasn't talking. She claimed she had given her word to the kidnapers that if she were treated well she would honor her end of the agreement by remaining silent.

The feds changed the tactic from good cop to bad cop. She was told she was one poor specimen of a citizen and not worth one hundredth of the amount her old man had forked over. She wasn't a GOOD AMERICAN. They thought they had finally broken her down when she tearfully asked to make a statement to the press. The media was quickly gathered. The cameras were hastily set up. All across the nation viewers leaned forward toward their sets so as not to miss one word of the frightening tale of abduction. A microphone was held out to Willie. She grasped it and made a heart wrenching appeal.

"Would somebody get me some food? I'm fucking starved."

An enraged interrogation team stepped up the intensity until a spokesperson from the American Psychoanalytic Association made a public statement that the interrogation was unconscionable. To force a person to face traumatic memories that they'd had to defensively repress would certainly result in permanent psychological damage and personality deformation. This stopped the de-briefing and Willie was forever grateful to the APA. She made a mental note to always give donations, when she became able, to their fund for destitute analysts.

The Attorney General knew this was all so much pure B.S. The girl had been brainwashed. Deposited now in her unconscious was an order that she would obey upon hearing a code word, like *baba ghanoush*. Then, like an automaton she would do the abominable bidding of her controller. Therefore, this girl must be kept under constant surveillance.

Whether this plan was carried out, we are not in a position to know, but years later, on her digs throughout the world, Willie sometimes noticed suspicious strangers jotting down notes just beyond the outskirts of her camp.

19

"Oh to be in the Arboretum now that spring is here," Byron paraphrased as he handed Cara her half of the foot-long turkey breast from Subway.

"I'm sure that's what Keats would have said if he'd been lucky enough to go to the U of M," Cara replied.

"Well done. An 'A' for the day."

"Surely not an 'A.' Much too elementary. I was expecting something like, 'We'll be as happy as birds in the spring.'"

Byron walked along chewing his sandwich and thinking furiously. "Ah yes, well I was going to say that next."

"And if you had, who would you have been?"

"I'd be Byron Page, happy to be contemplating marriage in three weeks to the greatest woman in the whole world."

"Think again, Dr. Page. That won't work. I've heard far too many handsome students like you try to worm their way past the simple fact that they don't know the answer to the question. This is a failing mark I'm putting next to your name."

"Ouch. Oh please, my father will cut off my allowance if I fail."

"All right . . . this time. But fair warning. Speaking of

which, I'm going to tell you something in the strictest confidence. I say this, not implying of course that you're a gossip, but only to impress upon you that the slightest leak about my plans would defeat the whole purpose of this action I'm about to take."

Byron recognized that Cara had become serious and was expecting a response—an agreement. "Cross my heart and hope to die," he said along with the appropriate crossing of his heart.

"OK, I've scheduled an inspection of the offices of the entire English faculty for this evening."

"You mean a raid?"

"That congers a picture of a SWAT team with weapons drawn."

"A raidlette, then."

"OK, if you must. Of course, I'm only expecting Schlink's office to yield evidence—possibly Sleeves's and Sheets's. But, if we only hit them, it will certainly give our suspicions away, besides all of the English faculty have motives."

Byron looked shocked. "*MOI*?"

"Even *tu*."

"And, when is this operation scheduled to come down?"

"Early evening, after the faculty has cleared out. No sense having irate professors shouting about their rights and getting in the way. To avoid that scary scene, I regret that I I'm forced to authorize overtime."

"Ah, 'Regret,' were all our public servants so civic minded."

Cara studied Byron's face for a moment. "I'm wondering why I told you about this. I knew you'd have to make fun of my plan."

Byron saw he had been following a playful line, not noticing that Cara was truly suffering from the lack of progress her investigation had made.

"I'm sorry. I was being my usual smart-ass self."

"I'm sorry too. I guess I'm jumpy."

"Aren't we a sorry couple," he said, grabbing her and kissing her.

It wasn't true that Cara didn't know why she'd told Byron of the raid. She'd wanted to give him time to protect any Shakespeare documents that might be seen by the investigating team. Her fellow detectives knew what was what in the world and would know the value of information like this. At the same time she didn't want to come out and say she was giving him an opportunity for concealment prior to an evidence-gathering raid.

After they parted, Byron was able to concentrate on the problem he faced. He had to get the box containing the crucial evidence out of Andy's office and he had to clear the three files from Andy's computer: the deleted e-mail messages, incoming file and the sent messages. He would have a very narrow window of time in which to accomplish this. He had to make sure that Andy left his office early. He thought of a plan.

On his way back to his office, Byron took out his cell phone and called Pam Backus and invited her and Andy for an impromptu dinner of his Welsh rabbit, a dish he could make after they'd arrived at his place. The time tolerance was very narrow. He was counting on Pam telling Andy to come home early to get ready. Even then, there would only be minutes to get to Andy's office and hide the evidence before the police raid and then race home before the Backuses pressed his doorbell. No one said a life of crime was leisurely. Byron sat in his office waiting hopefully for an early knock on his door.

It came. Andy opened the door and yelled out, "See you later, Wolfgang Puck." Then he was gone.

Byron didn't even check to see if a colleague was in the hallway. He went straight to Andy's computer and erased as needed, then grabbed up the "murder box," sealed it with tape and attached a label reading, "Notes, Faculty Meetings 1996-98." He was confident the box could stand in the corner of the faculty lounge for many years before anyone would open it. He had just deposited the box, when he heard a commotion outside—voices, shouted instructions and the tramping of a dozen feet. The time window had shut.

Byron came out of the lounge and walked straight to the stairs. As he opened the door to the stairwell he glanced back and noticed Hank Kelley standing before Andy's door as he waited for a member of the university's security staff to open it. It was at that moment that it first occurred to Byron that he would have to come back immediately after Pam and Andy left his house in order to get things back in place. Andy would be sure to dash to his office as soon as he learned of Cara's search operation. He would be compelled to know if the "murder box" was still safely in its hiding place.

Of course, the search produced no useable results for

the Ann Arbor Police, but they did turn up items in many of the offices that would provide hours of entertainment in the retelling during those boring hours on patrol. Andy must have been near a seizure until he was able to get back to his office and find his cube of textbooks intact, the box undisturbed. That alone would have accounted for the euphoria he displayed on entering Byron's house two days later, but Byron suspected there was an additional reason.

Andy practically floated across the threshold so high were his feelings.

"I've heard of a man feeling rejuvenation on a fine spring day, but you look like a man who's just discovered the joy of . . . golf sandals," Byron commented.

"You are looking at a published novelist. And, an unpublished novelist is to a published one as a trip to the moon is to getting back safely."

"I don't understand. Published? You said nothing to me about writing a novel much less submitting any work for publication."

"There is a distinct category of things one keeps to oneself until accomplished. Submitting a manuscript is one: having a hair transplant is another.

Andy walked back to Byron's dining room and made a circuit of the Sheraton table. He didn't know exactly where he was going as a matter of fact; the totality of his mind was on the fascinating story he had to tell of the way a mystery novel manuscript had been handed from one publisher to another, ending up with Cloistered Press, Byron's own publisher.

"Odd isn't it, but I suddenly feel a much deeper bond in our relationship, like we had blood ties," he said.

"A novel, huh? What's it about?"

"Surely you jest. You, who wouldn't give me the slightest hint about this Elizabethan scribbler—not that I care, you understand—but to think that you of all people would ask for advance information, well . . . it boggles the mind, that's what it does."

"Congratulations, then. But tell me, now that you're on the path to becoming a best-selling mystery writer, aren't you afraid that our murderer will include you on the list of the doomed."

"Odd thing about that: now that I'm one of them, I feel sympathy for them. They're not such a bad lot. I'm really sorry that I . . . that is, sorry that they . . . "

"I was only kidding," Byron said. He thought, "Well, well."

"This calls for a more festive drink than coffee," he went on.. I'll make an orange blossom. But we need more people. A cocktail party to celebrate; that's what I'll do."

Andy became sober. "If you're serious, I'd better break the news before the party. Another writer getting a book published is the kind of thing it takes an unpublished one time to digest, time to steady his or her social equilibrium before appearing in public."

Yes indeed, Byron thought to himself, we have evidence that it may be very indigestible to some.

"I see what you mean," Byron said. "This coming weekend I'll make an invitation list. Anyone you especially want me to invite, or especially to omit?"

"First of all, invite all of my enemies. I'm kidding. Invite as many and whom you please. The nice thing about success, it makes one feel so generous."

Byron was very pleased with what he was seeing before him, an immensely happy friend whose overflowing munificence might be expected to extend even to Dan Brown.

"I've brought muffins," Andy said. "So I think we had better stick to the usual coffee, this morning."

Byron got out a couple of plates and Andy put two muffins on each, then he sat and began to nibble on a muffin as Byron poured the coffee.

"I know insider trading is illegal in the stock market," Andy began, "But I don't think the law applies to your letting me in on the authorship and thereby enabling me—both of us actually—to make a little speculative profit. God knows I need it. My uncle didn't answer my last letter."

"What profit would that be?" asked Byron stirring sugar into his coffee.

"Like when a new inter-state highway is being planned, those who know the exact route can buy land adjacent to the interchanges."

Byron frowned, trying to relate this to his book about the author of the plays.

"Don't you see? The city the real Shakespeare came from will become an instant boomtown. His . . . "

"Or her—or don't you think of Elizabeth as a contender?" Byron interjected.

"OK, his or her birthplace could be bought for a song today, but after the book comes out . . . zoom goes the price. And then there's the old swimming hole where he . . . or she used to skinny-dip, and the hedgerow where he or she lost his or her virginity."

Andy snapped his fingers in excitement. "It would be worth a fortune to be the first on the market with the new dolls, T shirts, and after-shave . . . or the official reproduction of the real Shakespeare's quill pen."

Byron was shaking his head in disbelief.

Andy pressed on. "Loosen up man. Look I know you have this secrecy agreement with your publisher, but how about if I just name some candidates and you give me a signal when I'm right—say taking a bite of muffin? How about it?"

Byron considered this and said, "OK, I'll do it," and took a bite of his muffin.

"Not yet, damn it! Wait till I name someone. Now let's start with the obvious, Edward DeVere, Earl of Oxford. Ezra Pound says he's the man. So did Freud."

"Pam didn't make these muffins did she?"

"No, I bought them on the way over here, why?"

"They're not very good." Byron got up and dropped the muffin into the garbage can. "I was ready to go along with your proposal, but I can't now. These muffins are inedible, so I can't give you the required signal. Such a shame, the money we could have made. A chance of a life-time lost, all because you bought lousy muffins."

Of course Byron knew Andy had only been joking at breakfast—a cynical joke, as one might expect from Andy's long association with Henry Fielding. So naturally, Byron's first reaction to the call he got when he arrived at his office was to think it was Andy's extension of the same joke. The caller said he was Harvey Waltz and that he was the President of Comprehensive Marketing Associates. As he recited an impressive list of big names in the entertainment world he claimed as clients, Byron was trying to identify which member of the faculty Andy had enlisted into the prank. Gradually he recognized that the guy was making a real pitch.

"We handle the whole campaign. Not a minute of your time is demanded—after that first minute when you sign the contract. Everything: clothing, jewelry design and production, toys, board games, signature foods and drinks, tour groups, real estate, including the construction of hotels, a performing arts center and, of course, the many booklets, brochures and so on." Here he paused for dramatic effect before speaking the words he knew no normal person could refuse.

"Your share will be twenty percent of the net proceeds of all of our company's marketing of the new Shakespeare. We can offer this to you if we can learn the author's name immediately and be ahead of the field. The first one in is going to make the killing. I'm sure you realize that." He ended in a self-satisfied tone, "As the bard said, 'Put money in thy purse'."

"So he did," Byron muttered. To himself he thought that Harvey didn't know that he had just identified himself with one of the bard's most despicable characters, Iago.

"Mister Waltz, I know that what you've outlined is good business, but I can't join in it with you, because I have an understanding with my publisher that I will not reveal the name until the book is released."

"Hey, no problem. We'll cut him in for two percent. That will be two percent of, say about twenty million over the first ten years of the deal—four hundred thou. He'll jump at it. Besides, we will keep the identity of the author a strict secret until your book comes out. That, after all, is what guarantees our head-start."

Byron thought about this. He had lunched several times in New York with Howard Forsythe at the Harvard Club. Right now he visualized Howard, seersuckered, bow tied, having a watercress sandwich. The program Waltz had just suggested would prompt Howard's immediate need to lie down on one of the Club's leather couches. Still, he couldn't make a four hundred thousand dollar decision for another man.

"I'll call him, Mr. Waltz and relate your proposal."

"I don't want to give the impression that I'm pushy, Doctor Page, but time is of the essence. I'd appreciate it if you made that call today."

A few minutes later Byron was describing his conversation with Waltz to Forsythe, who confirmed that the man was everything he claimed to be.

"They market the whole secondary accessory paraphernalia for everyone from NASA to NASCAR, from film sagas to super athletes, pols to pandas. What he projects as a ten-year profit is probably conservative. Sadly, my answer will have to be no. I am aware that my not participating will not prevent this repulsive kind of commercialism. The moment the truth is known, they will flood the scene with all the articles Waltz described. I tend to follow Confucius's advice to relax and enjoy rape if it is inevitable—especially at the rate of two percent—nevertheless, I can't agree, because I have represented myself otherwise to my distributors and booksellers. Mr. Waltz may be sincere in the belief that he will be able to keep the secret, but there is no way in the world that it would happen. Someone pouring plaster to make a bust of . . . My God, I almost said the name over the phone. See how easily it happens."

"You're right, Howard. There would be a leaks."

"I'm sorry for you that I have to take this stance—no, I'm sorry for both of us—it's a lot of money."

"Howard, I knew this would be your position. Don't be sorry. As they say, we'll still be able to look ourselves in the eye when we shave each morning. But, come to think of it, I don't do that now, or I'd cut myself."

20

Tonight they were having borscht, just like his mother used to make.

"This is just like my mother used to make."

"Hush!" said Evita Lopez. "The maid might hear you. Don't forget, you're Latino."

Felix nodded and picked up his spoon and filled it with the rich, red soup.

"The police think the killer is Alonzo Schlink, an English Professor," stated Evita.

Felix lowered his spoon.

"Cornelia Washtenaw says that only if this is proven will the university have liability exposure."

Felix felt better and brought his spoon to his lips.

"But, if the police do manage to prove it, we're sunk."

Felix lowered his spoon.

"Cornelia says that four murders would max out the university's insurance. That, of course, would be the end of any hopes of your going on to be named permanent President."

Felix digested that thought and began to take a sip of the borscht.

"And, the end of our marriage."

Felix poured the soup out of the spoon and laid it on

the table. "Why is that, dear?" he asked in a whisper.

"Because you'll be forced to go back to Walnut College and I'll be damned if I will."

Evita's statement called up a vision of Walnut Junction, Ohio. Come to think of it, he didn't want to go back there, either.

"But, you say the police have no proof," he said hopefully"

"Yet. So far Doctor Schlink has been very clever. The police are sure it is he, but they have nothing they can take to court. One more author is yet to come here, however. The odds may catch up with Schlink this time. He may even be caught red-handed."

"I find that I'm not as hungry as I thought. Do you mind if I leave the table?"

"Suit yourself."

It was true that he had lost his appetite, but the real reason he left the dining room was to think. He sought the one room where he was assured of privacy. He lowered the lid and sat down to review the facts. If the situation could be frozen in time, the university was safe, his permanent appointment as presidency was still a possibility and his marriage would be saved. Alonzo Schlink must be prevented from attempting another murder. Alonzo Schlink must be removed from the U of M campus.

One week later, there was much activity outside the English Department Office. The mood of those milling about suggested that each had received news of an unexpected inheritance. The buzz was such that even the guessing game about the Shakespeare authorship had been put aside. They'd just heard the incredible news that Alonzo Schlink had accepted the Chairmanship of the English Department at Ohio State. For a year now O.S.U. had been desperately trying to get somebody—anybody—to accept the job. The crowd outside Henry Beasley's office, coffee cups in hand, was baffled. What could have possessed Schlink, a tenured professor at the University of Michigan, to do such a strange thing? What must he have demanded in order to coat this bitter pill for swallowing?

Joan Arnold knew of two of the demands; Sleeves had confided in her when he came in to empty his desk. Yes, Schlink had demanded that Sleeves and Sheets come with him, and be given tenured positions teaching only one class per week. That was readily acceded to. The second condition was more difficult for the hard-pressed Buckeyes. Schlink said that it was impossible to be associated with an institution given to such puerile, corny anachronisms as pretending that the tuba player is honored when he or she is chosen to dot the "i" when the marching band spells out "script" Ohio at halftime. The Ohio State Regents pouted like children who are no longer permitted to suck their thumbs, but in the end, they accepted Schlink's harsh demand. "Ohio" would no longer have a dotted "i."

"And they've gone already. Packed up their stuff and cleared out," said Andy to Byron, who had just arrived and didn't understand the cause of everyone's high spirits.

Byron thought of Cara. What would her plans be now that Schlink had fled her trap?

On the Ann Arbor Police GPS tracking system a blip was heading south on US 23, just having exited Interstate 75 at Findlay. The "bug" was in the heel of the left Bruno Magli loafer worn by Alonzo Schlink. In his pocket he carried a letter from Henry Beasley addressed to President Lopez. The same letter that had convinced him he had to leave the English Department at Michigan even if it meant—God forbid—Ohio State.

Life had been sweet for Schlink. He'd taught but one class a week to two somnolent grad students, had a sabbatical in view in two more years, a nice salary, and a professorship at the finest school in the mid-west. Plus Sleeves, Sheets and he had achieved a certain *cachet* with their "composite" novel.

Then there had come that fucking knock on the door. He'd gotten up from his desk and opened it. There stood this very fat, balding peasant with the bushy, crooked, black moustache, his face twitching. Schlink had thought, "My God, the marginal types. This is carrying equal opportunity too far."

"Professor Schlink, I'm the janitor, and I found this letter in the hall." The fat man held out a dirty, wrinkled sheet of 8 1/2 X 11.

Schlink noted several dirty footprints where it had been walked on.

"I was about to throw it in my waste barrel," the man gestured toward a wheeled cart such as Schlink had seen countless times in the building, "when I noticed your name and thought it might be something important you dropped." The fat man continued to hold the letter out to Schlink, who thought he'd better take a look at it if it, indeed, mentioned his name. He was also reluctant to touch the proffered filth.

"Ah, put it here on the desk."

The janitor complied, wished Schlink to "have a nice day" and left, closing the door after him.

Schlink saw that the letter was printed on the Department letterhead, Henry Beasley's name listed as Chairman.

"Dear President Lopez:

I hope that you appreciate by this letter that I intend to follow not only the letter, but also the spirit of your wishes for changes in the curriculum of the Department and also in the teaching assignments of our tenured faculty. I agree wholeheartedly that they must all assume greater responsibilities in undergraduate education. I believe as you do that the department must be put on a, to use your phrase, 'low fat diet.' The changes I am about to undertake will be department-wide, of course, but to give you an example I will cite the case of Professor Alonzo Schlink. Last quarter he taught but a two-hour seminar: 'The Metaphysical Poetry of Gerard Manly Hopkins.' Two graduate students were enrolled.

Next quarter, I am dropping this course from the curriculum and assigning Professor Schlink six sections of freshman English.

Working together, we can create, to quote you again if I may, 'a leaner meaner Michigan.'"

The signature looked like Beasley's all right.

Alonzo Schlink stared at the letter as he would a death threat. My God, even one section of freshman English would reduce him to babbling and drooling. Six sections! What could he do? Ten years before retirement age. He thought of suicide. Yes, he'd do that before teaching freshman English, but perhaps . . .

It was only at that depth of desperation that the possibility of the Ohio State chairmanship came to mind. He'd do it! He'd do it—but suicide remained an option.

. . .

The cocktail party was in its early, active, hopeful stage. Although most of the guests had been in contact during the week, here on a Friday evening, glasses in hand and in a context of presenting one's most desirable self, optimism prevailed. Laughter was quick and bright. Quips were truly clever. For a time the vows taken before leaving home to drink less, not say anything unkind and not talk too much about oneself, one's children, grandchildren and dog, were kept.

It wasn't until the second period of the party, the time at which information is sought on specific personal matters, such as, "Did Brent say anything to you about me and you know who?" that Ruth Hackett approached Byron as he stood alone mixing a Martini for Henry Beasley's wife, Laura.

"I was given a disquieting bit of information yesterday when I stopped by Campus Video to see if they had a DVD of *Nosferatu*. The clerk, a former student of mine, told me that two FBI agents had asked to see my record of film rental."

Byron stopped mixing and looked at her.

"Two agents, huh? Cara said they were compiling a profile of the killer."

"Well, I don't like it, I mean, why me? Or why any of

the other people they inquired about, for that matter?"

"What other people?"

"All of the women in the English Department. Didn't ask about a single guy."

"That's interesting."

"Interesting? If it had been your record they delved into, I think your reaction would be less composed."

Mischief suggested the next question to Byron. "What films have you been taking out? *Nosferatu* is about a blood-sucking vampire. How about *Silence of the Lambs,* was that on your list?"

"If I were to give you the list, you'd pass up the handcuffs and go for the straitjacket."

"Ruth, are you the murderer?"

"No, that is, I don't think so. Problem is, I'm so in sync with the killer's motives that at times I wonder."

"If you're not guilty, then you have nothing to fear. And, I doubt if they'll publish the list of films you've rented." Byron was trying for a reassuring tone.

"You're sweet. You mean well, but I don't think you believe for a minute that innocence is protection against a federal agency."

"You're right, actually I think you're in deep shit."

"Thank you. I like you better this way."

. . .

Cara received a summons to appear before the two federal agents. Special Agent Mann sat across the conference table from her. "Bunny" couldn't hide his excitement at the prospect of his big sister beating up on the kid who had called him names.

"As I said when we met earlier, this is a profile—an uncannily accurate and reliable construction—of the personality of the killer. We have reviewed the salient features of our composite and have compared the composite with the relevant persons in this case and have arrived at a name."

Here Twyla Mann paused and looked to Cara for a response. What was expected, Cara wondered—could it be applause?

"A name?" Cara repeated. She'd learned the technique in an early psychology course.

'The . . . ah . . . work required to fill in the details of evidence such as opportunity, method and so forth we leave to you. It's a matter of connecting the dots. You were, in grade school . . . .ah . . . able to connect the dots?"

"Yes, then and later. I have a shelf of trophies."

"All of our data points to a woman. Sleeping pills, bees, snowmen—the *operandi* of a woman. A man is more direct and violent: guns, knives, strangulation. In addition, as I hinted earlier, this person wants attention. She is someone who has felt passed-over, ignored, her worth not recognized. In her frustration she has resorted to fantasies of vengeful, violent retribution. She has been incited to these fantasies by the literature she reads and the depraved films she watches. *Road to Perdition* is an example. She, of course, has recently bought copies of at least one novel of all the writers scheduled to appear here in order to discover the themes upon which to build her exhibitionistic orgy of murder."

"Wow," Cara heard herself saying.

Twyla Mann approved of this response and delivered the reward.

"The murderer's name is Joan Arnold."

"Joan Arnold?" Cara gasped. "Byron and Andy's secretary? Incredible!"

"I'm not surprised by your reaction. Honestly now, you weren't even close to discovering this truth were you?"

"Honestly? Honestly, you're right; I never thought of Joan." She added to herself, "*And I hope no one ever thinks I did.*"

"Well?" The triumphant agent prompted.

"Naturally, we'll turn our attention now to Ms. Arnold. Thanks bundles for all your help. I suppose this means we won't have the pleasure of your company any longer?"

"That's so. We have to move on quickly to a *really* difficult case in Montana. Someone is rustling buffalo and transporting them across state lines. That, of course, makes it a federal offence."

Her voice serious, Cara said, "That person certainly made a terrible mistake. I mean doing that which would bring the pair of you into the case." She smiled a friendly farewell. "Happy buffalo hunting and . . . watch where you step."

21

The most famous of all antiquarian mystery writers stood on the podium and let her darkly outlined eyes fall as softly on her listeners as evening might settle on the Nile. Her hair, black as basalt, lay in two flat panels framing her oval face and continuing down to terminate in a straight line on her breast. She wore a simple amber shift with rounded neck and short sleeves. A gold snake band wound round her left arm above the elbow and a blue, faience amulet hung from her neck.

"'The non-anointed shall perish dare they open the *Book of the Dead*.'" The words seemed to hover in the room and then echo as if returning from the beginning of time.

"These words are inscribed on the wall of the Temple of Toth at Armana. Some scholars have read them as a warning. They are wrong." No one hearing her doubted that the scholars were wrong.

"This was no warning, this was a curse. It was taken down by the royal scribe, Nepseth, during the reign of Tutmose the Third." Here she touched the amulet with the tips of two fingers and then touched her lips. "It was dictated, of course, by Toth, the god of scribes."

Byron took a quick glance over the auditorium. All eyes were fixed on Isis; no one seemed to breathe.

"Since Poe, Wilkie Collins, and Conan Doyle first began the foolhardy practice of writing novels about murder, hundreds of violators of Toth's injunction have succumbed to unnatural death. Yes, *unnatural* death! In younger days I wasted much precious time looking into the details of their deaths. Wasted, because I should have known immediately what I would find. All mystery writers—except a sanctioned few—have died strangely. When one seeks out the details, one always finds—you may take my word for this—that in all cases Toth's hand was evident. The sanctioned few spared by Toth? The ones I've already mentioned plus Chandler and Sayers, Richard K. Morgan and . . . myself.

"This spate of death lately witnessed by all of you assembled here is evidence of Toth's impatient rage, his wish to bring an end to the coarse, commercial, irreverent and artificial parody of the sacred mystery of death practiced by the unworthy.

"Make no mistake, this is not merely his punishment you have witnessed, not merely the fulfillment of his curse. No! He has ordained these deaths to bring attention to the epidemic of sacrilege rampant in America today.

"I come here to bring a message to the young people in your university. JUST SAY NO! Say no to the temptation to write a mystery novel."

Elspeth Isis surveyed the audience with a sober, stern look. Suddenly, a radiant smile replaced the sternness and each person felt as if they were bathing in the beneficent warmth of Aton's love.

"I am also the bringer of glad tidings. It has been made known to me that Toth is satisfied that his message has been delivered. These deaths of demonstration are at an end. The non-anointed practitioners, the desecrators of *The Book of the Dead* will, of course, continue to end their days in agony, but this particular, well-publicized harvest is at an end. Rejoice in the name of Toth!"

She lifted her arms above her head, wrists together, hands splayed out. Many present thought they heard thunder.

No one applauded. It seemed inappropriate, like clapping at the end of a sermon. Elspeth returned to her seat on the podium. The podium had become a dais. One by one, in the order of rank, the faculty approached her to pay homage. Byron did also. He returned to sit next to Andy.

"She's nuttier than a fruitcake."

"Yeah, but like Barrymore, what a delivery."

Isis declined dinner. It had something to do with the passage of Osiris into the underworld. Byron and Beasley left the other faculty and escorted her to the hotel. Byron was aware of the figure of a fat man who flitted between the trees along their path and walked ahead of them on the other side of Thayer Street all the way to the hotel.

At the hotel, Elspeth Isis said goodnight. The lobby chairs were filled with very tough looking people. Isis nodded toward them and said, "It is a pity they will lose their sleep. There is really no need. I am completely safe." She smiled at Byron. "I think there is one among them who would better spend a precious night of her life in your arms than in anxiety for me. Tell her I will be well. Goodnight."

Byron was stunned. How could she know about Cara?

•   •   •

Sushi.Come was on North University around the corner from Byron's house. It was very popular at lunchtime and this meant that one usually had to wait for a table. Byron and Cara liked the bustle and the food.

It was now two days after the departure of Elspeth Isis and Cara finally dared to say, "I think we made it. I think the killing is over." She held up crossed fingers. "Over for good."

Byron said, "You believe, then, it's because Schlink is not here in Ann Arbor?"

She nodded, swallowing some sushi. "Not here, but also placated because he is now a department chairman—and too busy in his new job to take time out for murder."

"One would think a compulsive guy like Schlink might have wanted to finish a program he'd started . . . like writing the last chapter of a novel."

"It was a bad novel. Why, do you have a better theory to account for the survival of Isis?"

"Me? No, no. I agree with you. Placation. I like that."

Cara was smiling, both at the prospect of the end of the murders, but also because Byron supported her reasoning. "May he enjoy much success and placation at Ohio State, and if he has to resort to his old ways, at least it won't be on my turf."

Cara was also smiling because now there was nothing to interfere with the wedding and honeymoon, which was to be the day after Byron's book was released. Where they were going for a honeymoon was Byron's secret. He would only say that it wasn't England, because he was afraid of being met at the airport by a death squad from Stratford.

Byron lifted his cup of *saki*. "Here's to lasting success."

"Speaking of success, here's another example." She pointed to the headline of the *Michigan Daily* lying on the next table.

"Lopez named University of Michigan's 14th President." Under the headline was pictured a fat, broadly beaming, balding man. His posture suggested that he had suddenly stepped forward, partially blocking out the small woman standing next to him.

"I'm glad he made it," said Cara. "I think he's cute."

"Look, here's another familiar, smiling face," Byron pointed to a photograph and an article at the bottom of the front page.

"Professor Andrew Backus Hits A Double. The day after this popular English professor announced the publication of his first mystery novel, he received word that students had once again named him the English Department's favorite instructor."

"I think he's cute, too," Cara said.

"I'm jealous."

22

Byron's eyes opened to find Cara wrapped in a terry-cloth robe standing over him with a fresh cup of coffee.

"Rise and shine. Thought you'd like time to shower and brush your teeth with Ultra Bright. You're going to be doing a lot of smiling today."

Byron made a move at grabbing her hand and she stepped back. "No time for that."

"Those are the worst four words in the English language."

"You're very laid back. I wouldn't have been able to sleep last night if I were you. This is your big day, guy."

Byron stretched, then put both hands behind his head.

"You see, you've got it all wrong. It's not my big day, it's Shakespeare's big day. And, why should I be excited? I already know who he is."

"Hmm, I hadn't considered that. Well, whether you deserve it or not, you're going to be the center of a great deal of attention. You can receive that attention in your pajamas if you like, but since the camera will probably also catch me, I'm on my way to do the best I can to look good for my future children and grandchildren. I don't want them to have to make excuses for me years from now when they show their friends the pictures."

To Cara's back Byron yelled, "I didn't think you cared that much about what other people thought."

She was gone. Byron got up and headed for the bathroom. He'd been joking of course: this *was* a big day. Although he had made his discovery of a lifetime almost a year ago, this would be the day that defined him. Until now, it had been all the hard work he'd done as a scholar that had formed his professional identity. After today, those accomplishments would be forgotten. He would be known only as the discoverer of the author of the plays. And, any future scholarship, no matter how worthwhile, would be judged as the work of a man who had reached his peak and was now in decline.

He showered and dressed in jeans and a sweatshirt and ran down the stairs to the kitchen to drop a couple of pieces of bread in his expensive toaster.

He looked at the wall clock. 8:30. At noon precisely (5:00 P.M. Greenwich time) book dealers around the globe would open their package containing the special first edition and the cat would be out of the bag.

At 10:30 his friends began assembling for the walk to the downtown bookstores, first Andy and Pam, then Ruth Hackett, then Henry Beasley, even Hank Kelly. By 11:30 nearly the whole English Department including the graduate assistants filled the downstairs and flowed into conversational groups on the front porch and tiny lawn.

Byron looked at his watch and said to those standing around him, "The bookstores won't wait for us, so we'd better get rolling."

Byron, Cara, Andy and Pam, arms linked, led the

group now numbering two hundred.

"Somebody give Byron a flag to hold up so we won't get lost," came from somewhere in the crowd.

They rounded the corner onto North University, then right at State Street, filling the street from curb to curb and stopping traffic. Then after a left on Liberty, they saw another crowd ahead of them milling around the entrance to Border's. Byron noticed that some people, instead of entering the store were walking away appearing frustrated, even angry.

Holding Cara's hand he managed to move through to the door. There he saw what was causing the problem. A large notice was posted. It read: "The publisher of "Please Let Me Introduce Mr. William Shakespeare" is postponing the sale of the book until noon tomorrow. This is being done as a courtesy to the British who celebrate their Queen's birthday today."

Byron was stunned. With all the planning that had been done, they had failed to take into account that the English bookstores would be on holiday. He couldn't argue with the decision to postpone. After all, Shakespeare *was* English.

Byron turned to face all his friends. What could he do except shrug and say, "Well kids, I guess we'll just have to wait until tomorrow."

Printed in the United States
131842LV00002B/2/P

9 780979 852619